'That's Bates
coming up. 'H
hurt anyone a
he was drowne
them. The bac̲̲̲̲̲̲̲̲ drag him back
into the water. Maybe the poor blighter
couldn't swim.'

'He never had a chance. Look at his
head. He was either knocked out or killed on
the spot when that wave threw him against
the rock . . .' Biggles climbed up the sloping
side of the boat and looked down into the
cabin. 'Good grief!' he cried. 'Here's
another one.'

'Who is it?'

'Brunner.'

'Dead?'

'Looks like it. Wait.' Biggles scrambled
down into the cabin. He was soon back.
'He's dead all right,' he reported. 'But he
wasn't drowned. He was shot.'

About the author

Captain W. E. Johns, who died in 1968 at age of 75, served with considerable distinction in the R.F.C. in World War 1. After working with the R.A.F. in peacetime he became a prominent Air Correspondent and author of aviation books, and in 1932 he founded the magazine *Popular Flying*. Biggles first appeared in short stories in the same year, a character who was typical of the kind of man Captain Johns knew in the War.

Altogether Captain Johns wrote 85 books about Biggles, who has now become one of the most famous characters in children's fiction.

Biggles Sees Too Much

Captain W. E. Johns

KNIGHT BOOKS
Hodder and Stoughton

Copyright © 1970 W. E. Johns (Publications) Ltd.
First published 1970 by Brockhampton Press Ltd.

First published by Knight Books 1984
Second impression 1986

British Library C.I.P.

Johns, W. E.
    Biggles sees too much.
    I. title
823'.912[J]   PZ7

    ISBN 0-340-34513-6

Printed and bound in Great Britain for Hodder and
Stoughton Paperbacks, a division of Hodder and
Stoughton Ltd., Mill Road, Dunton Green, Sevenoaks,
Kent (Editorial office: 47 Bedford Square, London, WC1 3DP)
by Cox & Wyman Ltd., Reading.

CONTENTS

Chapter 1

A SMELL OF FISH

Air-Detective Inspector Bigglesworth, better known to his friends as Biggles, senior operational pilot of the Special Air Squad at Scotland Yard, tapped lightly on the door of the private office of his chief, Air Commodore Raymond, and without waiting for an answer looked in. 'Just to let you know I'm back, sir,' he announced.

The Air Commodore looked up. 'Come in – come in,' he said quickly. 'Don't run away. What's the hurry? How did you get on? Had a good rest?'

Biggles entered.

'How did you find that little place I recommended at Polcarron?' went on the Air Commodore. 'Sit down.'

'Just the job, sir,' replied Biggles. 'Exactly as you described it. Quiet, comfortable, plenty of good home cooking.'

'From the colour of your face you seem to have found a spot of sunshine, too. I hope you followed my advice and gave your brain a rest.'

Biggles smiled wanly. 'Matter of fact I found that a bit difficult.'

'What's that supposed to mean?'

'I'm afraid I've been running at full revs for so long, that I find it difficult to throttle back to dead slow.'

'I told you to forget everything to do with the office and anything to do with work,' chided the Air Commodore.

'So you did, sir,' agreed Biggles. 'But, as I say, that's easier said than done. I can't help thinking. It's become a habit.'

'What could you find to think about at an off-the-map spot like Polcarron, where nothing ever happens?'

Biggles cocked an eye. 'Doesn't it? I wouldn't care to bet on it. There may be other people who find a quiet spot has its uses. More may be happening on that pleasant strip of Cornish coast than one might imagine.'

'Such as what, exactly?'

'Possibly the answer to a problem that has had the Yard worried for some time. I said *possibly*. I can't produce concrete evidence to support that assertion. Well, practically none. But I did notice something that started my brain ticking over; and, as I say, once started I couldn't stop.'

'Go on,' requested the Air Commodore. 'What did you notice?'

'Purely by chance I saw some men going fishing.'

'What's wrong with that?'

'On the face of it, nothing. But again, purely by chance, I saw them come back.'

'What about it?'

'Simply this. The men who went to sea fishing were not the same men who came back. At any rate, not all of them. The number of fishers was the same, but something peculiar had happened to one of them. Naturally, from force of habit, I suppose, I began to wonder how this could have happened while the boat was on the water.'

'Come to the point,' ordered the Air Commodore.

'It suddenly struck me that there might be more to this fishing lark than meets the eye. It may have been the spot of bother that was giving the Press something to talk about when I went away that put my brain into gear for this particular train of thought.'

'And what was that?'

'There had been cases of illegal entry into the country You may remember on one notable occasion some coloured gentlemen, without paper of any sort, were found wandering inland from the south coast. They were unable, or refused, to give any account of themselves, where they came from or how they had got ashore. They were popped in the nick, and subsequently deported. Naturally, certain newspapers raised the question; how long had this sort of thing been going on and how many unwanted immigrants had slipped into the country by the same method? It was pointed out that this could be a danger to everyone.'

'Of course. They could have been refused legal entry on medical grounds, having got, or been in contact with, some killing disease like smallpox. I remember the case. Did you see any of these illegal immigrants in Cornwall?'

'No. But the thought occurred to me that sauce for the goose could be sauce for the gander and entry might not be confined to illegal immigrants. Now I'm pretty sure of it. In fact, I'll go so far as to say that a full-scale racket, in this particular line of crookery, might be going on under the noses of the police, coastguards and Excise men. As you know, I've had quite a bit to do with smuggling in one form or another, but this transport of human freight would be something new. And there could be a lot of money in it for the organisers.'

The Air Commodore was frowning. He sat back in his chair. 'I take your point,' he said thoughtfully. 'It could be very profitable. But how is it being done?'

'As I see it now, nothing could be easier.'

'I asked you *how*.'

'By these fishing trips out to mid-Channel. I'm talking in particular of these shark-fishing exercises that apparently have become quite big business on the south-west coast. But don't get me wrong. I have no doubt that the majority of people in the game are absolutely genuine, honest and above board; but if one, just one, was a wrong 'un, he could do a lot of mischief.'

'You're dead right,' returned the Air Commodore grimly. 'Strange that nobody seems to have thought of it. What put the notion into your head in the first place?'

Biggles hesitated. 'It's rather a long story.'

'Never mind. You might as well get the whole thing off your chest while we're at it.'

'If you say so, sir,' answered Biggles. 'It all came about like this. You know Polcarron, so that makes it easier. It's not much more than a hamlet; a dozen or so cottages occupied by men who for generations have managed to make a living from the sea; inshore fishing, a few lobster pots in the season and a little boat building when the weather is bad. The harbour itself is nothing to shout about; a stone quayside and a short mole built out to provide protection for a few small craft. The people don't bother, or haven't the equipment, for this shark-fishing pastime. That's mostly done from the larger places further along the coast, St Mawes, Falmouth, and so on. I, personally, hadn't the slightest interest in it. I've seen all the sharks I ever want to see.' Biggles broke off.

He continued. 'Having had my breakfast, with nothing to do, I made it a practice to stroll down to the quay and make myself comfortable on a wooden bench where the old salts sometimes gathered to talk about the good old days when life was easier – or so they seemed to think. It amused me to listen to them. One old man would always drift along, so I got to know him quite well. His name was Sam. Sam Pretty. Once in a while a coastguard would roll up to join in the conversation. Where he came from I don't know; some nearby station, I suppose. As it was of no importance to me I didn't ask him.' Biggles paused.

'One fine morning I was sunning myself on the seat listening to old Sam – he always did most of the talking – when a powerful-looking motor-boat came in and tied up to the wharf. I suppose one could call it a launch – a sort of cabin cruiser. It was the first time I'd seen it. Sam, who knew most things, informed me it was one of these shark-fishing outfits. It came in from time to time to pick up clients who presumably found Polcarron a handy place for embarkation. There was a crew of three on board. They didn't come ashore. They sat on deck, apparently waiting for someone. Sure enough, presently a chauffeur-driven Daimler came along and four men got out. They went aboard the boat, which then cast off and headed out to sea. The car also disappeared. I had no real interest in all this, but after things had returned to normal Sam opened up on this new shark-fishing sport.

'I gather it is fairly expensive. It isn't necessary to provide your own tackle. You simply book a boat that specialises in this sort of pastime and the skipper does the rest. That is, he brings the rods and the bait and heads out to where he knows sharks are most likely to be found, which Sam said was about twenty miles out in the Channel. You pay by the hour. Having seen sharks fairly close in, I asked why it was necessary to go so far. Whereupon Sam informed me these sharks I'd seen were common basking sharks, quite harmless and no

good for sport. The real fighters stay further out. Sam
went on and I listened. I still wasn't really interested.
Frankly, I couldn't have cared less. In fact I found it
somewhat boring, but once my salty old chum got
under way on a subject, there was no holding him. I
learned that quite a ceremony has grown up around this
sharking industry. When the boat comes back, if a fish
has been caught, it flies a signal to mark the event. Two
fish, two signals and so on.'

'So now you know all about it,' put in the Air
Commodore. 'What do they do with the fish they
catch?'

'I don't know,' confessed Biggles. 'I didn't bother to
ask. As I say, all this was no concern of mine. If people
can get a kick out of hooking a shark they can have it.
That's all right with me. Every man to his taste.
Anyhow, that's how I got my education on the new
sport of shark-fishing. I went back to my pub and forgot
all about it.'

'You seem to have picked up quite a lot,' remarked
the Air Commodore.

'You'll think so by the time I've finished,' promised
Biggles. 'You've only heard the half of it.'

'Carry on, then, and let's hear the rest,' suggested the
Air Commodore.

Biggles obliged. 'After lunch, as the sun was still
shining and I had nothing better to do, I went back to
my seat. Sam who had told me he always took a nap
about this time, wasn't there. I sat and looked at the
sea, and nearly went to sleep myself. However, I pulled
myself together when I saw the shark fishers coming
back. I noticed the signal to show someone had been
lucky. A shark had been caught. I watched the boat
come in and tie up at the same spot against the wharf.

Four men came off. At the same time the Daimler cruised in to pick them up. It all went like clockwork. The four men got into the car and off it went. That was the last I saw of it. The boat cast off, and that, too, disappeared round the headland to the west. That was the end of the entertainment.'

The Air Commodore looked disappointed. 'So that's all there was to it?'

'Not quite. Indeed, far from it. It was about now that I caught my first smell of something fishy. And it wasn't shark I could smell.'

'What caused the aroma?'

'I told you that four men got out of the car and went on the boat. I didn't pay any particular attention to them, but I'm sure they were all clean shaven. Had it been otherwise I would have noticed it. Four men went fishing and four came back.'

'Is there anything remarkable in that?'

'Yes. They were not the same men. At least one was different; that I'm prepared to swear. He had a beard. How did that happen? The fellow could hardly have grown whiskers in the five or six hours the boat had been at sea. Pondering the matter I could arrive at only one conclusion. Somewhere in the Channel there had been a switch; a swop with a man from another boat.'

The Air Commodore, with his eyes on Biggles' face, was looking more and more serious. 'Did you get the number of the car?'

'No.'

'Why not?'

'When it was there I hadn't the slightest interest in it. My brain only got weaving after it had gone and I had time to think. I don't go around taking the number of every car I see.'

'All right – all right. There's no need to get snooty,' admonished the Air Commodore. 'Did you get the name of the boat?'

'No. For the same reason. I only woke up after it had gone. Later I did ask Sam where it came from. He didn't know. He could only point vaguely along the coast, which might mean any one of the score of harbours, large or small, between where we were sitting and Land's End.'

'Would you recognise the boat if you saw it again?' asked the Air Commodore.

Biggles shook his head. 'I doubt it. There are probably hundreds like it round the coast. I'm no sailor, having spent more time over the ocean than on it. All I can say is, it was a well-built job looking as if it was intended for salt water.'

The Air Commodore nodded. 'I can see what's on your mind. You think someone is using a small boat to bring in people who, for one reason or another, realise they couldn't get in any other way.'

'Why not, if they have the money to pay for it? Somebody could be making a nice thing out of it. When you come to think about it, what could be easier? A boat goes out, ostensibly shark-fishing, so nobody takes any notice of it. Well clear of the coast it makes contact, probably by appointment, with another craft from the French side. The switch is made and the shark outfit returns to England. I don't see what's to stop it.'

'There are such people as coastguards.'

'I doubt if there are enough to cover our two thousand miles of foreshore, all day and all night throughout the year. The crooks would know where they were, we may be sure of that; their regular beats and when they come on and off duty. In any case there must be a limit to what can be expected of a coastguard or Excise man. He sees four men go fishing. That must be going on all the time. He sees four men come back. He might search the boat. What does he find? Fish. What other check has he? You can't expect him to photograph all these men, or take fingerprints, to make sure that the ones who went out are the same as those who come back, even if the thought occurred to him. It wouldn't be practicable.'

'Are you suggesting all this shark-fishing is a blind? A cover to engage in smuggling unwanted immigrants into the country?'

'Of course not. One crooked outfit would be enough to cause a lot of trouble. A fish or two could be brought home once in a while to make the trip look genuine.'

'This boat you saw. Did it bring home a shark?'

'It was making a signal to show that it had caught one.'

'Did you see it?'

'No. I didn't look for it. One wasn't brought ashore, so presumably the anglers didn't want it. What can you do with a dead shark, anyway? This shark-fishing is supposed to be a sport, not fishmongery.'

'Why are you so sure that a racket is going on?' enquired the Air Commodore curiously. 'From what you've told me I can see the possibilities, but that's a long way from proof. Why are you convinced?'

'I thought I recognised one of the men who came ashore. It hit me suddenly, after he'd gone. The fellow with the beard. There was something vaguely familiar about him. I felt sure I'd seen him before somewhere. It wasn't the beard that gave him away. That would disguise his face, but it couldn't hide an infirmity. A limp. He dragged one foot, I've just checked up with the records and now I'm sure I wasn't mistaken.'

'Who was it?'

'Logan. Known to his gangster pals as Limpy. Limpy Logan. A gunman. You must remember him. He was shot in the leg in a night-club brawl, in Soho, years ago. He once ran a protection racket. Later he specialised in hijacking commercial lorries on the motorways. Eventually the police caught up with him and he got a stretch of five years. Eighteen months ago he escaped from Wormwood Scrubs and was never caught. It's my guess he got abroad and has been there ever since. Now, deciding it's safe, the fuss having died down, he's come home to rejoin his associates or perhaps collect some money he had tucked away somewhere. He wouldn't be so daft as to risk recognition at any regular port of entry, sea or airport. But you can take it from me he's here. Limpy Logan is back in circulation. The underworld will soon get to hear of it.'

The Air Commodore was frowning. 'I don't like the sound of this,' he muttered.

'I knew you wouldn't,' returned Biggles. 'Naturally, one begins to wonder how long this has been going on; how many villains have got in and out of the country the same way. It's a safe bet that this is a two-way traffic.' Biggles shrugged. 'Well, sir, there it is. You asked me what was on my mind. Now you know.'

'Something will have to be done to stop this racket,' declared the Air Commodore.

Biggles ghosted a smile. 'That's what I expected you to say, sir. Now perhaps you'll do the talking and tell me how you propose to spot one particular boat among the thousands that jam every mooring between Land's End and John o' Groats. Sailing is a national pastime.'

The Air Commodore considered the matter. 'I'll

speak to the Chief Commissioner and get his views,' he decided. 'You, too, can think about it and put forward a suggestion. I realise it wouldn't be easy to find that boat, but if we have patience it may come to us. I mean to Polcarron. If it has used that harbour once, it may use it again.'

'Limpy Logan isn't likely to be on it. He's already here.'

'Never mind about him. I can deal with that. I'll notify all stations to keep an eye open for him. It's more important that we should put a stop to this illegal entry racket, and the only way to do that is to catch the man who's behind it. For the moment it might be a good idea if you extended your holiday at Polcarron for a few days, keeping your eyes on the harbour and your ears to the ground for local whispers.'

Biggles' smile broadened. 'That suits me, sir. The pub has a good line in crabs and lobsters, which are right up my street. May I take somebody with me? Too much of Old Sam would get boring.'

'Certainly. Take who you like. But don't rush off today. Think about it. Work out a scheme. I'll see you again before you leave. But I don't think an aircraft will be much use to you in this case.'

Biggles looked surprised. 'On the contrary, I can't see how we could do much without one.'

It was the Air Commodore's turn to raise his eyebrows. 'Why not?'

'Well, to get a conviction we'd have to catch these smugglers in human freight red-handed. It wouldn't be much use trailing them in another boat. They'd spot they were being watched and there wouldn't be any smuggling that day. They'd keep clear of their confederates from the French coast. But it's unlikely they'd take any notice of a plane passing overhead. From the air it should be possible to watch the entire operation and jump on the boat when it returned home. Of course, the whole thing would be simplified if we knew the boat we were trying to catch, otherwise we might spend a lot of time shadowing innocent parties.'

'Yes, I see that,' agreed the Air Commodore. 'All right. I'll leave it to you to make what arrangements you like. But let me know what you intend to do before you start.'

'I'll do that, sir. Just one last thought. I wouldn't say anything yet to the Coastguard or Customs Service. They could be brought in when we're ready. If they knew what was afoot, it would be natural for them suddenly to be on the alert, in which case the word would go round and the gang would get to hear of it. They would then either lay off altogether for a while or take extra precautions, which wouldn't make our job any easier.'

'Very well. You can rely on me to keep the whole thing under the hat, for the time being, at all events,' promised the Air Commodore.

'Thank you, sir. Now, I'll get organised.' Biggles left the room.

Chapter 2

A WAITING GAME

A week after the conversation in the Air Commodore's office, Biggles was again lounging on the seafront bench at the little harbour of Polcarron. Keeping him company was police pilot Bertie Lissie. They had in fact been sitting there on and off for three days, and for all the good they had done they might as well have stayed at home. Bertie was getting bored with gazing at the same unchanging scene and made no secret of it. Even the coming and going of the few local 'crabbing' boats with their meagre catches of crabs and lobsters had become monotonous.

'Patience,' advised Biggles gently. 'We knew when we started this was likely to be a waiting game played slow. You're having a nice holiday and being paid for it. What more do you want? No doubt Algy and Ginger are getting a bit bored, too.'

'This bally seat gets harder every day,' complained Bertie.

'Go buy yourself a cushion,' chaffed Biggles.

Although he did not say so, he was himself getting a little tired of watching the ever-restless ocean and the same few men and their boats that used the little harbour for their lawful purposes. Of the motor-boat he had hoped to find there had been no sign, and a casual reference to it, to old Sam Pretty who joined them every morning, elicited the negative information that he hadn't seen it either since they had both seen it come in to

pick up the party of shark fishers. He knew the boat but
had forgotten its name, which was unfortunate, for this
information would have saved a lot of trouble. Biggles
did not pursue his questioning in case the old man, who
was anything but a fool, became suspicious of their real
purpose there. So they had no alternative than to wait
for it to appear, on the assumption that if it had used
Polcarron once, it would sooner or later use it again.

Two days spent exploring the near-by coast had been
enough to reveal the futility of trying to locate one
particular boat, not even the name of which was known.
In Falmouth harbour, for instance, one of the largest in
Europe, there were craft of every description, both large
and small. Here alone a short excursion was sufficient
to show there were scores of places where a boat could
tie up or drop an anchor without calling attention to
itself. Not only in the main harbour. The River Fal and
its tributaries ran inland for miles, even as far as the city
of Truro. Apart from the river there were numerous
secluded tidal creeks in which even great ocean oil
tankers could find a safe berth when not in use. Some
were provided with landing facilities. As a matter of
detail, the size and depth of some of these waterways
can be judged by the fact that they were large enough to
hide part of the invasion fleet that assembled in
readiness for D-Day in the last world war.

Biggles wondered why, with all these mooring
facilities available, the boat he sought should make use
of a small harbour like Polcarron. Could it be on
account of the coastguard station overlooking the
entrance of the port of Falmouth, a position from which
every vessel coming or going could be watched?

He had made inquiries about a prospective shark-
fishing trip, but here again he found there were more

small boat owners engaged in the sport than he had imagined. As the weather was fine, most of them were at sea, anyway, and so could not be interviewed. Some of them advertised openly, and these, he thought, could be ruled out.

Here again he dare not ask too many questions for fear of arousing suspicion as to the purpose of them. Anyhow, for these reasons he decided that the only safe plan would be to wait at Polcarron for the boat he wanted to reappear, although this might take time.

For the rest, the arrangements he had made to deal with the situation were as uncomplicated as possible. He and Bertie would keep the little harbour at Polcarron under observation. They had come down in Biggles' own car, the old Ford Pilot, which now stood parked at the end of the quay. A few miles inland, at the Morven Flying Club aerodrome, near the village of that name, Algy and Ginger were standing by with the Auster of the Air Police Flight. All they had to do was wait for the radio signal from Biggles that would send them into the air to shadow the boat under suspicion. This was assuming the boat would come into the harbour. From there it would be followed out to sea and a check kept on its movements. Biggles and Bertie would, of course, watch anything that happened ashore. As Biggles was aware, there were weaknesses in this plan, but he thought that, apart from unforseen circumstances, it should work.

Biggles had elected to do the watching at Polcarron because he was the only one of the party able to recognise the motor-boat should it appear, although it must be admitted he was by no means sure of this. As he had told the Air Commodore, his knowledge of such craft was limited.

Radio contact could be made at any rate between the two parties by means of portable short-wave equipment, which in Biggles' case hung from a strap over his shoulder. Being in a leather case, it might have been taken by a passing stranger for a camera or a pair of binoculars, both of which are commonly carried on seaside holidays. Apart from testing the radio to make sure it was functioning properly, there had as yet been no reason to use it, so as Biggles remarked to Bertie, Algy and Ginger were no doubt also becoming more than somewhat bored with so much time on their hands and nothing to do except listen for the call signal.

This is how matters stood as we found them in their usual positions on the quayside bench, Biggles smoking his customary cigarette and Bertie, with the local daily paper at his feet where it had fallen, half asleep in the warm sunshine.

Suddenly Biggles became alive. With his elbow he gave Bertie a hefty poke in the ribs. 'Here we are,' he said tersely. 'Look what's arrived.'

Bertie looked, and saw a large black car coming to a stop a little further along the quay, actually at the foot of the ramp that formed a sort of slipway to the road above.

'A Princess,' he murmured. 'Is that the one you saw?'

'I wouldn't know,' Biggles answered. 'I imagine so. There can't be many of 'em in a place like this.'

Nobody got out of the car, but a man in a peaked cap could be seen sitting at the wheel.

'What do you suppose he's doing?' asked Bertie.

'If he *is* our bird he should be here to meet someone,' replied Biggles.

'Shark fishers off the boat?'

'What else?'

'Where's the boat?'

'Obviously it isn't here yet, or we'd see it. If this is an appointment, something seems to have gone wrong. Either the car is early or the boat is late.'

'The car hasn't brought anyone here, so it must have come to pick up somebody.'

'That's what it looks like,' agreed Biggles. 'I've got the number of the car. You'd better memorise it, too. Get ready to move. When it leaves here I want you to follow it to its destination, wherever that might be.'

'What about you?'

'I shall stay here to see what happens. I'll give Algy the signal if the boat shows up. It doesn't need both of us to follow the car. I'll leave that to you.'

'Okay. Shall I move off now?'

'No. Wait for the car to go. Hello! What's he doing?'

The driver of the big car had got out and with binoculars to his eyes was either adjusting them or scanning the seascape.

'He's looking for the boat,' guessed Bertie.

'My scheme seems to have gone cockeye,' stated Biggles. 'I reckoned that the car, when it came, would bring a passenger. It looks as if it has only come here to collect someone.'

The next development was the last thing he could have anticipated. The chauffeur cased his binoculars, strolled along the quay and joined them on the bench. 'Could you oblige me with a match?' he asked Biggles civilly, producing a packet of cigarettes.

'Sure,' answered Biggles, offering his lighter, which gave him an opportunity to have a good look at the speaker without making his scrutiny conspicuous.

He was a rather small middle-aged man, clean shaven with a lean face, high cheek bones and dark, deep-set eyes that had a penetrating quality about them. His nose was slightly misshapen, flattened, as if he had been involved in an accident, or perhaps had been a boxer.

'Thanks,' acknowledged the man, returning the lighter. 'Down here on holiday?' he went on, casually, a natural remark in the circumstances.

Biggles nodded. 'For what other reason would one be here?' he said whimsically.

'Staying at the local pub?' was the next question, as if to make conversation.

'Of course,' Biggles had to admit, for as far as he knew there was no other accommodation.

'Ever do any fishing?'

'Can't say I have.'

'Good way of passing the time. Besides, if you're lucky you get fresh fish for breakfast.'

'Is that why you're here?' enquired Biggles blandly.

'Not me; my boss is dead keen on it, though. Pretty good at it, too. He's out there now.'

'What does he catch?'

'All sorts, although his latest craze is shark-fishing. Seems they give you a hard fight.'

'So I would imagine,' Biggles said dryly.

This conversation had been carried on in a manner so natural and congenial that no offence could be taken at the questions, or the answers.

The man glanced at his wrist watch. 'He's late today,' he went on. 'He should have been in by now. I was here to meet him. The sport must be good to keep him, unless they're having trouble with the engine.' He stood up and looked out to sea. 'I don't see him coming, so I might as well be having a pint while I'm waiting. So long.' The chauffeur walked away in the direction of the little hotel.

'Well, what do you make of all that?' Bertie asked, when the man had gone some distance.

'That's what I'm wondering,' answered Biggles. 'There could be more than one answer.'

'You're sure it's the same car you saw last time?'

'Almost certain, although I couldn't swear to it. Of course, that fellow may be perfectly innocent, and doesn't know what his boss is really doing.'

'You don't believe that,' challenged Bertie.

'No, frankly I don't. He struck me a cool customer. If you want my opinion, I'd say he saw us sitting here, and wondering who we were and what we were doing in a place like this, came along to have a close look at us. To ask for a light for a cigarette is always a reasonable excuse to get into conversation. I believe he must have been telling the truth when he said his boss was late back, otherwise he wouldn't have brought the car here yet.'

'Unless part of his job is to come early for a scout round to make sure the coast is clear,' suggested Bertie.

'You could be right, at that,' conceded Biggles.

'And now, having given us a once-over, he's gone along to the pub for a drink.'

'He may have a pint while he's there, but if you asked me to guess his real purpose, I'd say he's gone to get our names from one of the hotel staff, or from the visitor's book on the hall table.'

'Would it matter?'

'It might. That could depend on how far back he looked in the book. Don't forget the Chief has often been here. That's why he was able to recommend the place to me. My name might mean nothing, but if our amiable chauffeur friend is a crook, he'd almost certainly have heard of Air Commodore Raymond of the Yard, in which case the game would be up as far as we're concerned. We wouldn't see that car for dust.'

'That's a sobering thought, old boy,' returned Bertie, seriously. 'What can we do about it?'

'Nothing, that I can see.'

'The Daimler is still here.'

'It'll be interesting to see how long it stays here. I imagine that whatever the chauffeur may think he'll have to wait for his boss. There's no need for us to get in a flap. We'll stay where we are. The drill is the same. When the car goes you do your best to follow it.'

Bertie was gazing out to sea. 'I can see a boat coming now. Looks like a fast motor-boat from the wake it's churning up. Seems to be heading in this direction.'

'I see it,' Biggles said, looking. 'The chauffeur will spot it, too, from the pub, no doubt. Yes, here he is, coming back, presumably to be on the spot when the boss arrives. He seems to be in a hurry.'

'Then why is he getting into his car?'

'To move it nearer to the landing stage, I suppose.'

'No. That isn't the answer. It looks as if he's moving off altogether.'

'By thunder!' exclaimed Biggles, staring. 'I believe you're right. Off you go. Get after him. I'll watch what happens here. Buck up or you may lose him.'

Bertie strode briskly towards their own car.

Chapter 3

LUCK WORKS TWO WAYS

In no small perplexity Biggles watched the departure of
the Daimler followed not too closely by Bertie. He
couldn't understand what was happening. What was
going on? The chauffeur was there to meet his boss. He
had said so himself, and as that was expected there had
been no reason to think otherwise. Yet now, with the
boat, presumably the one he had come to meet, in sight,
he was leaving? In fact, he had gone. What had caused
the chauffeur to change his mind? What had gone
wrong? What *could* have gone wrong? Up to this point
everything had worked out according to plan, yet now,
with the departure of the Daimler, the bottom seemed
to have fallen out of it. Biggles was bemused and
bewildered.

With his brain racing in top gear, he turned his
attention to the oncoming power boat, still too far out
for details to be observed. What he saw only made his
confusion worse. It had changed direction and was now
on a more westerly course. For a moment he thought,
and hoped, this was merely to avoid an obstruction; but
he soon saw that this was not so. The boat, throwing
behind it a foaming wake of white water to show the
speed at which it was travelling, held steadily on its new
course. It was evident that whatever port it was making
for, it was not Polcarron.

When he realised this, Biggles was assailed by a
feeling of frustration and helplessness. It looked as if the

boat had in some way been warned to keep clear of
Polcarron. How had that been done? Who had done it?
Something must have happened, for the boat had
certainly been heading for Polcarron. The chauffeur of
the Daimler must have known about the change of plan.
That was why he had gone instead of waiting on the
quay as had obviously been his original intention.
Could the chauffeur have had some hand in this?
wondered Biggles, thinking fast.

One thing, he realised, was all too apparent. He had
missed the boat. Literally as well as figuratively. And
without transport there was nothing he could do about
it. To try to intercept the boat by travelling on foot was
obviously out of the question. Already it was out of sight
beyond the headland to the west of Polcarron. It would
have reached one of the ports farther along the coast
long before he could get there. To look for it among the
scores of other small craft would be futile.

For the same reason it seemed pointless to call up the
plane on the radio. Algy and Ginger would need a few
minutes to get into the air; and when they reached the
coast, how were they to recognise one particular craft
among the many that would be on the water in
harbours or close inshore?

No, that was no use, Biggles thought helplessly. He
had been outwitted, he told himself bitterly. But how –
how – how, was the question that hammered in his
head. He sank back on the bench. All he could hope for
now was that Bertie would have better luck with the
Daimler. After a minute or two, impotent, but feeling he
might as well be doing something instead of seeking
inspiration in the sea, he made his way along the quay
and up the ramp leading to the road and his hotel,
appropriately named The Fishermen's Arms.

He found the usual man serving behind the bar. By this time, as a resident he was on familiar terms with him. He ordered a glass of beer, and while the barman was drawing it asked casually: 'Tell me, Tom. Did a fellow in a chauffeur's uniform come in here a little while ago?'

The answer, as he expected, was 'Yes.'

'Do you know him?'

'No. He's been in once or twice, but I don't know his name.'

'What did he want?'

'A whisky – soda.'

'Did he ask any questions?'

'He asked if we had any spare rooms.'

'What did you say?'

'I told him the truth. We only had two and they were taken. I don't think he believed me, because I saw him go to the hall and look at the visitors' book. He must have seen your name, because when he came back he asked me how long Bigglesworth and Lissie were staying here.'

'What did you say?'

'I told him you'd booked for an indefinite stay.'

'Then what?'

'That was all. He lit a fag and strolled over to the window. Then he finished his drink in a bit of a hurry and went out.'

'How did he light his fag?'

Tom looked surprised by the question, as he had reason to be. 'He had a lighter. Why?'

'I just wondered.' Biggles smiled lugubriously as he sipped his beer. That answered one question, anyway. When the chauffeur asked him for a match, he had a lighter in his pocket. Clearly, he was making an excuse to speak, and perhaps have a closer look at the two men sitting on the bench. A common enough excuse, and reasonable. So he had been suspicious. Why? The answer to that was not hard to find.

Still sipping his beer Biggles began to see a glimmer of daylight. After speaking to them the chauffeur had gone to the pub, ostensibly to get a drink, but really to find out if he and Bertie were lodging there. At the same time he had learned their names. Would the name Bigglesworth mean anything to him? Biggles wondered uneasily. It might or it might not. If it had, its association with Scotland Yard would account for what had followed. Somehow the man had made a signal to the boat. Evidently he was wide-awake. Equally evident, he was in the racket; or engaged in something illegal. His behaviour was not that of an honest citizen on holiday.

Biggles finished his beer. 'I'll be back presently for lunch,' he told the barman over his shoulder as he went out to return to the quay, there to await Bertie's return. Of course, he had no idea of how long he would be.

It so happened that he had less time to wait than he expected. Within half an hour he saw him coming down the ramp. He stopped at the bench and got out; and even before he spoke Biggles knew that things had not gone well.

'Well, how did you get on?' he asked.

'I lost him,' announced Bertie dejectedly.

'How did that happen?'

'You know what some of these sunken Cornish lanes are like, winding about up and down hill with never a view on either side or far ahead. I managed fairly well for a time, although without getting too close, it wasn't easy to keep him in sight – if you see what I mean. Then sheer rotten luck stepped in. A farmer opened a gate just in front of me and let a herd of cows pour into the road. I had to stop. I was held up for a good five minutes and that was that. Where the Daimler went I don't know. I dashed around for a while but couldn't find it. Never saw it again. So I had to pack it in.' Bertie held out his hands. 'What else could I do?'

'Nothing,' Biggles answered shortly. 'Did the fellow in the Daimler realise you were tailing him?'

'I don't know. It wouldn't have made any difference. He had nothing to do with those bally cows, anyhow.'

Biggles nodded. 'Apparently this isn't our lucky day.'

'Why? Did something go wrong here?'

'Very much so.'

'What happened when the boat came in?'

'It didn't come in.'

Bertie blinked. 'It didn't?'

'It did not.'

'Where did it go?'

'I haven't a clue. It changed course and shot away somewhere to the west. Without transport there was nothing I could do about it. I'm no marathon runner. It passed out of sight behind the headland, going at a rate of knots.'

'I was sure it was heading for here!'

'So it was. The man in charge changed his mind, and I think I know why. Somehow our chauffeur pal gave him the tip to keep clear. I haven't much doubt about that. I've been to the pub and turned up one or two interesting little facts. You'll remember the chauffeur went there when he left us? I can now tell you he went there to make some inquiries about us. I'm afraid he got the information he wanted. If I'm right, let's face it, this morning, one way and another, we've done more harm than good. We've shown the enemy our hand and got nothing in return. We shall now have to do some hard rethinking.'

'Tell me, old boy. What did you find out at the pub to make you so sure of all this?'

Biggles narrated briefly what he had ascertained at the hotel, and concluded: 'If, as we have reason to suspect, the man driving the Daimler is a crook, one of the gang that has been operating from here, it's almost certain that he'll know me by name, and what I do for a living. Well, now he knows. You realise what that means? They'll give this place a wide berth, at any rate while we're here. We may have to find fresh quarters for all the good we shall do here. I may be wrong. We shall see. Now the damage has been done there's no need to do anything in a hurry. We might as well go up to the pub and tear a lobster to pieces.'

'Have you told Algy about this?' asked Bertie.

'Not yet; but I shall have to.'

'Why not now? Better let him know right away how things stand with us, so that he'll be ready for a quick change of plan – if you see what I mean?'

'It might be as well,' agreed Biggles, unstrapping the case containing the radio.

He was soon in touch. 'It's Ginger,' he told Bertie in a quick aside. He spoke again. 'What were you saying? I'm listening.'

It seemed to Bertie that he listened for a long time, with only an occasional interjection that conveyed nothing to Bertie, who sat watching. When he saw that Biggles had switched off he said: 'Perhaps you wouldn't mind telling me what all that was about.'

'It may be that we haven't entirely wasted our time after all,' answered Biggles, buckling up the radio equipment. 'At least, we now know the answer to the mystery as to why the boat changed course. We also know the name, or the nickname, of the gent driving the Daimler. It's Pug Bates.'

Bertie's eyes were saucering. 'How on earth do you know this? What could Ginger have had to do with it?'

'Plenty,' replied Biggles. 'Listen and I'll tell you. The luck hasn't all been against us. We've had a spot of it, too. An hour ago Ginger tried to get in touch with us to find out if we had any news. Twiddling the knobs he cut in on another radio conversation coming through. There was some interference, but he got the gist of it. Someone named Pug Bates was warning someone to keep clear of Polcarron because two Yard men were watching the harbour. So now we know. That must have been the chauffeur talking to the boat. He had a pug nose. Evidently the Daimler is fitted for two-way radio. It's all so simple now we know the answer. We might have guessed it. Of course, the conversation Ginger had butted into by accident meant nothing to him and he only mentioned it to me to explain why he hadn't been through to us before. But it means a lot to us.'

'I noticed an aerial on the Daimler, but I assumed it was just the standard car radio,' Bertie said.

'Naturally, you would,' returned Biggles. 'It begins to look as if we're up against a more efficient organisation than I had imagined. There must be big money in it for them to go to all this trouble and expense. But that's enough for now. There's nothing we can do for the moment, so we might as well have some lunch. This afternoon we'll slip along and have a word with Algy and Ginger. They'd better know how things stand.'

'At least we know the registration number of that bally Daimler,' reminded Bertie.

'That's something to go on with,' stated Biggles. 'We'll find out who it belongs to. That shouldn't take long.'

Leaving their car where it stood, they went up to the road and crossed to their hotel on the opposite side. Pushing open the glass-panelled swing doors into the hall, they were passing on to the dining-room when Biggles paused to look at the small side-table where the postman regularly put any mail. 'Just a minute, here's a parcel for me,' he said to Bertie. 'At least, it's addressed to Captain Bigglesworth, so I can only suppose that means me. Seems I've been promoted. It can't be from the Air Commodore. Who else would write to me here?' He picked up the small, compact parcel. 'Feels heavy,' he remarked.

'Let's have a dekko.' Bertie reached for the parcel. Between them they fumbled it and it fell on the uncarpeted floor.

Biggles stopped and picked it up. Suddenly he stiffened, and with a curious expression on his face he raised the parcel to an ear. 'Must be a clock. I can hear it ticking,' he told Bertie, who was watching all this with questioning eyes. Then he moved. Fast. Dashing to the end of the hall, he flung open the swing doors, and after a swift glance up and down for possible traffic, he hurled the parcel to the far side of the road. It struck the sea wall and bounced back on to the pavement that skirted it. Simultaneously there was a shattering explosion. The packing material flew in all directions, and from the spot where the parcel had struck the ground, a thin cloud of blue smoke drifted into the air.

The blast had sent Biggles staggering back. He

bumped into Bertie who had followed him out to see what he was doing.'

'My sainted aunt!' gasped Bertie. 'What a stinker! Good thing you didn't waste any time with it.'

Biggles' face was pale under its tan. 'Had I stopped to open it, Tom would now be picking up pieces of my face off the floor,' he said grimly.

'How did you know what it was?'

'I didn't know. I only suspected. The address made me suspect it was phoney before I picked it up and felt the weight of it. Lucky we dropped it, so we can't complain on that score. That triggered something off. I could hear ticking. I wasn't taking any chances. I couldn't get rid of the thing fast enough. I might have been wrong. As it turned out I was right. Well, now we know how far these villains are prepared to go. Let's go back and have a drink. I need one. That was a close shave, close enough to shake me.'

When they went to the bar and ordered drinks Tom said: 'What was that bang I heard? It rattled the windows.'

'Must have been some silly ass barging through the sound barrier,' Biggles suggested casually. 'By the way, there was a parcel for me in the hall. Do you know how it got there?'

'No. I didn't see it arrive,' Tom said. 'Couldn't have been the postman. It isn't his time.'

'Never mind. Forget it,' returned Biggles, carelessly. 'If lunch is ready so am I. Come on, Bertie. Let's go through.'

'I seem to have lost my appetite,' Bertie remarked as they sat at their regular table.

'Oh come, now,' bantered Biggles. 'You're too experienced a soldier to let a little squib like that upset you.' Then he added seriously: 'We've had a warning, so from now on we shall have to watch how we go. The gang we've crashed into don't believe in wasting time; and it looks as if they're prepared to take a little thing like murder in their stride. I'm puzzled as to how that parcel got in the hall. Did the chauffeur come back here, or is there a member of the gang always stationed here?'

Bertie shook his head. 'No use asking me, old boy. No use at all. No doubt, as some wizard once remarked, time will show.'

Chapter 4

BIGGLES MAKES SOME INQUIRIES

Biggles was quiet over lunch. Bertie, realising he was preoccupied with the events of the morning, did not interrupt his thoughts. However, when they had finished their meal, over coffee Biggles said: 'You must be trying to work out what's on my mind. I'll tell you. I'm wondering if it's any use staying on here now the enemy knows who we are. Let's not fool ourselves. They must also have a pretty good idea of *why* we're here, or they wouldn't have planted that bomb this morning. Of course, that chauffeur wasn't really looking for rooms when he came here. He merely wanted to find out who we were and how long we intended to stay. Let us put it this way. Is it any use our staying here now these racketeers know all the answers? At least, we can assume they do.'

'They'll soon know their effort to bump us off didn't work. All the same, they'll suppose it gave us a fright and they'll expect us to move to healthier quarters,' opined Bertie pensively.

'I was thinking on the same lines,' returned Biggles. 'So what's the answer? I've usually found it pays off to avoid doing what is expected of me. As you say, they'll expect us to clear out: therefore I feel inclined to stay put, which should give *them* something to think about. It'd be risky, no doubt. Having failed to eliminate us at the first attempt, doesn't mean they won't have another go.'

'Absolutely, old boy, absolutely,' murmured Bertie.
'But it goes against the grain to give 'em the impression
that they've got us scared.'

'They've got me scared all right; don't get any wrong
ideas about that,' confessed Biggles grimly. 'But after
what happened this morning the matter has become
personal. When people have a crack at me I get a strong
impulse to hit back at 'em. I'm nothing for turning the
other cheek, or any nonsense of that sort. In my
experience it's likely to hurt more. The trouble is, we
still haven't a clue as to who's behind this racket. They
have the advantage of knowing who we are. But given
time we should be able to get that sorted out.'

'We know one man who must know who they are – if
you follow me,' Bertie pointed out.

'Who?'

'Limpy Logan; if you're right in thinking you saw
him smuggled ashore.'

'We don't know where he is.'

'If the police could pick him up we could ask him a
few pointed questions.'

'He wouldn't squeal.'

'He might, if we turned the screws on hard enough.'

Biggles shook his head. 'I wouldn't care to rely on it.
We've got to find him first, anyway. There is one other
thing that might give us a lead. We've got the number of
that Daimler. We'll ask the Yard to let us know who it
belongs to. That shouldn't take long. I don't feel like
telephoning from here. Let's go and put Algy and
Ginger wise to the latest development. I'll phone the
Yard from a post-office, or when we get to the
clubhouse. When they've got the answer they can call
me back.'

'Will you tell the Chief what's gone on here?'

'Not on your life. With the best of intentions he'd probably order us to return home, and maybe take us off the case altogether. I don't want that to happen. When I get my teeth into something I hate having to let go. But let's press on and see the boys. We've left my car unattended long enough as it is.'

They left the hotel, and having made sure they were not being followed returned to the car. It was still where it had been left, and as far as could be judged from a quick inspection, they were satisfied that it had not been interfered with. Having warned Bertie to keep an eye open behind them to check if they were being shadowed, Biggles set off for the aerodrome. A drive of half an hour saw them at their destination, where they found Algy and Ginger standing by the aircraft.

Biggles said to them: 'Now we're here there's no need to wait for signals. I've something to tell you. Let's go over to the clubhouse. I have to make a phone call to the Yard. You can wait for me on the veranda. I shan't be long.'

When they reached the wooden building Biggles went on to the secretary's office. He was away a few minutes. When he returned, taking a seat he said: 'They're going to ring me back here when they've got the information I want, so we can take our time.'

Then, for the benefit of Algy and Ginger, he related what had happened at Polcarron that morning. He concluded by saying: 'That's how things stand at the moment. We thought you had better know the position right away.'

'So what do we do now?' enquired Ginger, looking concerned.

'I haven't made up my mind yet,' Biggles answered. 'It depends on what the Yard is able to tell me about that Daimler. I can hear the phone now. It might be them.'

'Your call,' cried the Club Secretary.

Biggles departed. He was away a few minutes and came back folding a slip of paper, which he put in his wallet. 'I've got the information I wanted,' he said, resuming his seat.

'Tell us,' requested Bertie.

'It's not exactly what I expected,' Biggles said. 'The Daimler belongs to a Mr Julius Brunner, who lives at Penlock Grange, which is not far from Polcarron, as I've just ascertained from the map in the office. As a matter of fact I noticed a signpost pointing to the village of Penlock on the way here, so I know roughly where it is.'

'Brunner. That name rings a bell,' put in Bertie.

Biggles continued. 'Apparently, he's one of these international financiers who have a finger in all sorts of pies. One of his interests is a chain of hotels, on the Continent as well as in this country.'

'Does he own a power boat?' asked Algy.

'If he does, the Yard didn't mention it. Perhaps they wouldn't know. Of course, if he has one it needn't necessarily be registered in his own name.'

'Hold hard,' put in Bertie sharply. 'I've just remembered where I saw the name Brunner. It's over the door of our pub in Polcarron. I've seen him about once or twice, but I've never spoken to him. He lives over the hotel. I once heard him speak to Tom, the barman. He has a bit of a foreign accent.'

'It isn't the same man,' stated Biggles. 'I noticed the name on the registration plate over the door of The Fishermen's Arms. It's Stephen Brunner. The man who owns the Daimler is Julius Brunner.'

'Is that a coincidence?'

'Could be. He might be a relation, a brother, perhaps. We'll find out what hotels Julius owns. Come to think of it, a chain of hotels would be useful in the sort of business we suspect Julius really runs. I mean, they could be used to accommodate people he picks up at sea. I agree the names are too much of a coincidence to be ignored.'

'If Stephen at The Fishermen's Arms is in the racket,' said Bertie, 'it may have been he who planted that box of tricks in the hall this morning.'

'I hadn't overlooked that possibility,' replied Biggles. 'But this is all guess work,' he went on. 'Let's get some facts. Tom, the barman, should know if the man who runs our pub is any relation of Julius Brunner. After all, he's in the public house business himself. But we shall have to be careful about how we ask questions. Tom may know something about the racket that's going on, even if he isn't in it himself, which is not impossible. I don't trust anybody these days.'

Ginger broke in. 'Whether he is or not, I reckon the sooner you shake the dust of The Fisherman's Arms off the soles of your shoes, the more likely you are to live a bit longer.'

'You may be right,' concluded Biggles. 'But the man who runs our pub has no reason to suspect how much we know. I feel like hanging on to have a good look at him. If he's in the racket, it shouldn't be long before he gives himself away.'

'Yes, by putting a spoonful of arsenic in your soup,' stated Ginger with cold sarcasm.

'We shall have to do our best to see that doesn't happen,' returned Biggles evenly. 'I may have second thoughts about staying on at Polcarron; but let's not argue about that now. I suggest we go and have a look at Penlock Grange, from the outside of course. We can all go. Let's get weaving.'

As they all went to the car Biggles went on. 'I think you'd better drive, Algy.'

'Why?' asked Algy, looking surprised, for it was customary for Biggles to drive his own car.

'We're going into what we'd better regard as hostile country,' Biggles answered. 'If Bertie and I sit in the back, we're less likely to be seen by the chauffeur of that Daimler should we bump into him, as might happen. We must reckon he lives at Penlock Grange, or in the village.'

'I get it,' Algy said, taking his place at the wheel.

Ginger sat beside him. Biggles and Bertie sat in the rear seat and in that order they set off.

Biggles guided Algy back down the road he had taken to reach the aerodrome, as far as the signpost he had mentioned; but after that the ground was new to all of them. However, by following the road for two or three miles through typical Cornish countryside, they came to the village of Penlock, as was revealed by the name over the post-office-cum-shop. Here the road forked. So far there had been no sign of a big house that might be The Grange.

'Now where?' asked Algy.

'Stop here,' ordered Biggles. 'Before we take the wrong road and lose ourselves. I'll step into the village shop for a packet of cigarettes as an excuse to ask the way to The Grange; otherwise we might wander about for hours without finding it.'

Algy brought the car to a halt.

Biggles got out and walked the few yards back to the post-office-cum-shop. To the elderly woman behind the counter he said, 'Packet of cigarettes, please. Any sort will do.' Then, as she reached to a shelf behind her for the cigarettes, he went on. 'Am I going right for Penlock Grange?'

'Straight on. Take the left fork and you can't miss it,' was the polite answer. 'It's about half a mile. You'll see the iron gates at the entrance to the drive.'

'Thank you,' acknowledged Biggles, picking up the cigarettes and paying for them. An afterthought struck him and he continued. 'Is there anywhere here where one could put up for a day or two? I'd like to stay here for a little while.'

The woman answered. 'Mrs Cator sometimes does bed and breakfast for hikers in the summer. That's at Fernside, the cottage at the far end of the village, on the right.'

'Thank you,' Biggles said again. 'Good morning.' He went on. Or rather, he moved to go out, but the door was pushed open from the outside and he collided with a man coming in. A man in uniform. It was the chauffeur of the Daimler. In the collision a letter he was carrying fell to the floor. In a flash Biggles had stooped and picked it up, address side uppermost. 'So sorry,' he said, as he handed it over.

As the two men looked at each other, it would be hard to say who was the more surprised. For a moment the chauffeur looked startled, an expression that was not missed by Biggles, who was the first to speak.

'So it's you,' he said smoothly. 'Well – well. So we meet again. What are you doing here?'

'What are *you* doing here?' enquired the chauffeur in a brittle voice.

'Oh, just having a jaunt round to look at the landscape as a change from the sea,' explained Biggles. 'Nice part of the country. Do you live in these parts?'

'Me. No fear. I was just passing through and stopped for a packet of cigarettes.'

'Same as me,' Biggles said, smiling.

'You still staying at Polcarron?' enquired the chauffeur.

'Yes, I see no reason to move,' replied Biggles.

'Be seeing you again then, perhaps.'

'I hope so.'

The chauffeur went on to the counter. Biggles noticed he was evidently a regular customer, for the woman handed him a packet of cigarettes as if she knew the brand he smoked; which of course gave the lie to his denial that he lived near. He did not wait to renew the conversation, but returned to his car, passing the Daimler on the way.

'Sorry about that,' said Algy. 'There was nothing I could do about it. The Daimler came round the bend and pulled up tight against me.'

'Okay. Drive on,' answered Biggles shortly.

'I don't think he saw me,' put in Bertie. 'As soon as I saw the Daimler coming I bobbed down.'

'Unfortunately he saw me,' returned Biggles. 'There was no avoiding it. I was coming out as he came in and we bumped into each other. We had a few words.'

'What did he come in for?'

'A packet of cigarettes; also, I think, to buy a stamp for a letter he had in his hand. I managed to get a glimpse of the address. At this moment he's probably asking the postmistress what I came in for. If she tells him I came in to ask the way to The Grange, that should give him something to think about. If, in addition, she tells him I asked about lodgings in the village, he won't be long reporting it to his boss.'

'Why did you ask her that?'

'I had ideas of staying here for a while; but in view of what's just happened, I shall have to think twice about that. Unless our chauffeur friend is a fool, which I doubt, he'll realise I wasn't there by accident.'

'What was the address on the letter he came in to post?' asked Algy.

'It was addressed to Mr S. Brunner, Fishermen's Arms, Polcarron,' stated Biggles succinctly. 'And that gives *us* something to think about. It pretty well confirms what we suspected. There's a hook-up between The Grange, here, and The Fishermen's Arms. Take it slowly, Algy. According to the woman in the shop there are iron gates at the entrance to the drive leading to The Grange. Here they are, on the right. They've been left open, for the Daimler, I imagine. Don't stop, but slow down enough for us to see up the drive.'

'The Daimler's coming up behind us,' informed Bertie after a glance through the rear window.

'Carry straight on, Algy,' ordered Biggles. 'Don't slow down.'

They carried on for perhaps half a mile. Then, on Biggles' orders, the car was brought to a stop. 'We'll wait here,' he said. 'If it doesn't pass us we'll know the Daimler turned up the drive. To make an excuse for stopping, get out and open the bonnet as if you're having trouble with the engine.'

Algy did this.

When they had waited for five minutes and the Daimler had not appeared Biggles said, 'Okay. That's all we want to know. It must have turned up the drive. No doubt the chauffeur was in a hurry to get home to report to his boss that we were in the village.'

'So what do we do now?' asked Algy.

'Cruise back as if we've discovered we were on the wrong road. We'd better not hang about here in case we're being watched.'

'How about dropping me off to have a prowl round?' suggested Ginger. 'Nobody knows me, so it wouldn't matter if I was seen.'

'I don't see why not,' agreed Biggles, after considering the proposal. 'You get out and walk back. We'll wait for you in the village. But for goodness' sake be careful what you get up to. Don't take any chances. These men are dangerous. They've demonstrated that.'

'Okay.' Ginger got out.

Algy reversed the car and took it back over the road they had just covered, towards the village. They passed the iron gates. They were now closed. A bend in the drive cut off any view of what lay beyond.

'When we get to the village, stop outside the pub,' Biggles told Algy. 'I saw one as we came through. We might be able to get a cup o' tea. I could do with one.'

Algy drove the car to the village inn. A few drops of rain from a passing storm were now falling, so they sat in the car until it had cleared.

They were glad to learn that the proprietor did 'Teas in the Garden' and were soon seated round a table with one of the renowned Cornish teas in front of them. They did not hurry over it, expecting Ginger would be some time. They had plenty to talk about. But when an hour had passed and Ginger had not appeared, Biggles announced that he was getting worried.

After another hour of waiting he said: 'I don't like this. What can he be doing? I can only hope he hasn't landed himself in trouble. We can't leave the car standing outside here any longer, or people will begin to wonder what we're doing. Don't forget what I said about us being in hostile country.'

'What else can we do except wait?' asked Algy.

'There's one thing we might do,' Biggles replied. 'Bertie could drive you back to the aerodrome. I'll wait here. When he's taken you home he can come back here for me. Ginger should be here by then. If he isn't, we shall have to find out why. We can't push off leaving him here.'

'That means making two journeys to the aerodrome, taking Ginger there,' Bertie pointed out.

'Why not? We're in no hurry.'

'Okay, if you say so, old boy,' agreed Bertie. 'Come on, Algy, I'll waffle you home.'

They departed, leaving Biggles alone. Presently, for something to do, he paid the bill. He then returned to his chair in the garden.

Chapter 5

COMPLICATIONS

Although it was now the twilight of sunset, Biggles was still sitting in the garden of the public house when Bertie returned, alone, of course, having dropped Algy on the airfield as had been arranged.

Bertie looked around. Not seeing Ginger he said: 'Isn't he back yet?'

'Not a sign of him.'

'You haven't heard anything of him?'

'Not a word.'

Bertie looked serious. 'What on earth could have happened to him?'

'I wouldn't even try to guess.'

'This isn't like him. He must have run into trouble.'

'I'm afraid that's the only answer.'

'What can we do about it?'

'Not much, as far as I can see.'

'Do we stay here, or do we go back to Polcarron for the night?'

'If we go back to Polcarron and come back here in the morning, if he's run into trouble the position will be the same as it is at this moment.'

'Where could he have gone?'

'He might be anywhere.'

'The Grange?'

'It's not much use going there to make inquiries. If he is there, they wouldn't be likely to tell us. If he isn't there, the answer would be the same. They'd deny all knowledge of him.'

'I see what you mean,' Bertie said pensively. 'Is it any use going to look for him?'

'In the dark? Not a hope.'

'We can't just push off leaving him to his own devices, as they say – whatever that may mean.'

'One of us might stay in case he turns up,' Biggles said. 'Even if I could find lodgings, and the post-office told me of a woman who sometimes lets rooms, I couldn't arrive, without it looking queer, without any sort of luggage; not even a rucksack.'

'Yes, I see that,' agreed Bertie. 'But if you feel like staying here, I could slip back to Polcarron and fetch your small kit; just the essentials, if you follow me.'

'It's an idea,' Biggles conceded. 'I'll tell you what. You wait here while I slip along to Fernside, the cottage where the woman lets rooms, to find out if she can fix me up with a bed. A Mrs Cator. If she can't, that settles the question.'

'Fair enough, old boy, you do that,' Bertie said.

Biggles got up. 'You wait here, I shan't be long. By the way, I've paid the bill.' Biggles departed.

He was back in five minutes. 'That's okay. I've fixed it,' he reported. 'Mrs Cator has only one single room, so she can't put up both of us. You go back to Polcarron and fetch my kit. You can get as much as I shall need in the haversack. Be as quick as you can. When you've brought my stuff, you'll have to go back to Polcarron for the night and come back here for me first thing in the morning. You'll find the cottage about a hundred yards along. The name's on the gate.'

They left it at that. 'Be seeing you,' Bertie said, and hurried off.

He wasted no time returning to Polcarron. It was of course quite dark by the time he arrived at The Fishermen's Arms. As he would soon need the car again, he did not put it in the hotel garage, but left it close to the front door. It took him only a few minutes to collect Biggles' pyjamas and toilet things and pack them into his haversack. He was on his way out when the thought struck him; to save the hotel staff unnecessary trouble, it was only right that he should warn them that he might be in late for the evening meal and that he would probably be alone. Thinking Tom could take the message to the kitchen, he turned into the bar. Tom was not there. To his surprise he saw his place had been taken by a man he had never seen before. A slim, swarthy fellow who certainly looked anything but English.

In the circumstances he asked the most natural question. 'Where's Tom?'

'Gone,' was the laconic answer, with an accent that confirmed he was not English.

'Gone! Gone where?'

'He's left.'

'You mean – left altogether?' Bertie was astonished.

'Yes.'

'That was a bit sudden, wasn't it?'

The new barman shrugged. 'He walk out.'

'Extraordinary thing to do after being here for so long,' Bertie said. 'He said nothing to me about leaving. Ah well; I suppose he had his reasons.'

'They come and go,' said the man behind the bar, polishing a glass.

Bertie went on. 'I only looked in to say I might be late in for supper. You might let them know in the kitchen.'

'I tell. You want drink?'

'Not now. I'm driving.'

More than a little puzzled Bertie went out. But deciding the sudden departure of the old barman was no concern of his, by the time he had got into his car and started the engine he had dismissed the matter from his mind. He drove off. He had got no further than the last street lamp, a matter of not more than a hundred yards, when his nerves were jolted by a voice close behind him. Obviously from the back seat. He brought the car to a skidding stop beside the kerb and looked round.

'It's all right, sir. It's me. Tom,' said the voice.

'What are you doing in my car?' demanded Bertie, annoyed by the delay.

'I was hoping to have a few words with you, sir, in confidence.'

'Why here?'

'I didn't want anyone to see us talking.'

'Talk? What about? The new man in the bar told me you'd just walked out at a moment's notice.'

'That's a lie. I was fired,' stated Tom in a hard voice.

'How did that happen?'

'The Boss came in, gave me a week's wages in lieu of notice and told me to get out.'

'He must have had a reason. What had you been up to – fiddling the till?'

'I don't do that sort of thing,' declared Tom coldly. 'He said I talked too much.'

'To whom?'

'I don't know. You and Mr Bigglesworth, I suppose. Who else is there to talk to? The locals don't talk much to me.'

'When you say the Boss, who do you mean?' enquired Bertie, now taking an interest.

'Mr Brunner.'

'The man who owns the place; lives upstairs.'

'He doesn't own it. He runs the pub for another man of the same name; a Mr Julius Brunner; a relation, I fancy, as they seem to be pretty thick when I've heard 'em talking on the telephone.'

'I see,' murmured Bertie, thoughtfully. 'But what has all this to do with me? Do you want me to take you somewhere?'

'No thanks. I've managed to find a room in the village for the time being; till I can find another job.'

'Then what *do* you want – money?'

'No. It isn't that. I can manage for a while. I wanted to ask your advice.'

'Well, carry on. But make it quick, because I've got to get back to Mr Bigglesworth.'

'There's something queer going on at The Fishermen's Arms. And I told 'em so.'

'Told who?'

'The Boss.'

'That wasn't very clever of you. I'm not surprised you got the sack. What do you mean queer?'

'These comings and goings at all hours; all very secretive. Queer people. All colours. I don't like the look of some of 'em. They never talk to me. They come and they go. Maybe I only see 'em once. A shifty-looking lot. Usually come in twos or threes. Never go out. They can't be ordinary people on holiday, because they never have any luggage when they arrive, although I notice they've usually got a suitcase when they go. Another thing. They don't leave in the clothes they come in. Somehow they look quite different. You don't see this because you're nearly always out. I was wondering if I ought to tell the police. What do you think?'

'How long has this been going on?' asked Bertie.

'Must be some five or six weeks now.'

'And how long have you been barman at The Fishermen's Arms?'

'Close on seven years. I was with the previous owners before this lot took over the place.'

'When did that happen?'

'About six months ago. It happened sort o' sudden. I didn't know anything about it. I wasn't even told the place was up for sale. I was simply asked if I'd stay on under the new management and of course I said yes. Anyhow, I thought I'd give it a trial. Now I don't like the look of it. The place ain't what it used to be. Somehow the old atmosphere has changed. The takings at the bar have gone down. That wasn't my fault. I haven't changed. I still do my job. This new man, Brunner, must be losing money; yet the strange thing is he doesn't seem to mind.'

'Tell me honestly, what do you think's going on? You must have formed an opinion.'

'I'd say some sort of smuggling racket. That's only my guess, but I can't think of anything else. I fancy that's why they sacked me. I saw too much. Brunner knew that.'

'How?'

'The other day I asked him straight out who all these people were who came and went the next day. He told me to get on with my job and mind my own business. The trouble started from then. He decided to have me out and here I am. If you were in my place, would you go to the police and tell 'em there's something mighty odd going on at the pub and say it was time they had a look at it?'

By this time Bertie was wondering if he should take

Tom into his confidence and tell him who he really was and what he was doing in Polcarron. He decided against it. It was too soon. It might do more harm than good. Moreover there was just a possibility that Tom was a spy acting for the enemy; that all this was a trick to find out how much he knew or suspected.

Therefore he said: 'If you're asking my advice I'll give it to you. If I were you I'd say nothing to anyone. Keep your mouth shut about what you suspect. You talk too much and you might find yourself in worse trouble.'

'Perhaps you're right,' Tom said thoughtfully. 'Are you staying on at The Fishermen's Arms?'

'For a day or two, anyway. I'll keep in mind what you've told me. Where are you going? I mean, where could I get in touch with you if I wanted to speak to you?'

'I shall be staying for the time being at one of the cottages along the front. Number eight. A widow woman named Mrs Berry lives there and sometimes takes lodgers.'

'I see. I may call on you one day to see if you know anything more about The Fishermen's Arms. Anything you say will be safe with me. Now I must press on, or Mr Bigglesworth will be wondering what I'm doing.'

'Right you are, sir.' Tom got out. 'Good night, sir.'

'Good night, Tom.' Before driving on Bertie snatched a glance through the rear window to check if he was being watched. He saw a figure step back quickly into a shadow. He wasn't sure, but he thought it was the new barman at the hotel. For a moment he wondered if he should warn Tom to be more careful because he had been seen getting out of the car. But Tom was already walking away, so he did nothing about it, a decision he was shortly to regret.

With his head full of what Tom had just told him, he drove on. He had no doubts as to why Tom had been given the sack. Stupidly he had revealed that he suspected something underhand was going on at the hotel. Biggles, he thought, would be interested in this latest development.

When he reached Penlock, knowing that Biggles would no longer be at the inn, he went straight to his lodging, Fernside Cottage. Taking the haversack he went to the door and knocked. It was opened by an elderly woman.

'Mrs Cator?' questioned Bertie.

'Yes, that's right.'

'I believe you have a friend of mine staying here, a Mr Bigglesworth. I've brought his luggage; just the things he'll need. I might as well have a word with him while I'm here.'

'I'm afraid you can't do that.'

'Why not?'

'He's gone out.'

'Oh!' For a second Bertie was nonplussed by this unexpected piece of information. 'Do you know where he went?'

'No.'

'Did he say how long he'd be?'

'No.'

'He didn't leave a message for me?'

'No. He just said it was a fine night so he'd take a stroll for some fresh air. I haven't seen him since. I've been expecting him back any minute, because I told him I usually locked the door at ten o'clock, when I go to bed.'

'It's nearly that now,' Bertie said.

'Yes. I'm waiting to lock up.'

'Well, here are his things. You might put them in his room.' Bertie handed over the haversack. 'I'll wait outside for a bit. I don't suppose he'll be long.'

'Won't you come in?'

'No thanks.'

'Just as you like. If he's late he'll know you've been from his things being here.'

'Thank you.' Bertie returned to the car and sat behind the wheel. He was surprised that Biggles, knowing he was coming, had gone out. He couldn't think why. He was even more surprised that he had not left a message saying how long he'd be. It was true he himself had taken longer on his trip to Polcarron and back than had been estimated, due to the conversation with Tom. Had Biggles got tired of waiting?

Bertie sat slumped in his seat. He was tired and somewhat bored. He found all this hanging about, doing nothing, tiresome. He waited for nearly an hour, by which time most of the lights had gone out and a rural silence had settled on the village. What to do for the best he didn't know. He became annoyed that Biggles should keep him waiting like this. To try to find him in the dark, not knowing in which direction he had gone, would obviously be a waste of time. Anyway, he reflected, when Biggles did return he would hardly expect to find him still at Fernside Cottage.

He waited until eleven o'clock and then decided there was only one thing for him to do unless he was prepared to spend the night in the car. If he was not soon back at The Fisherman's Arms he was likely to find the door locked. When Biggles did return he would find his small kit in his room, so he would know he had called. Far from happy he started back for Polcarron.

He arrived just in time to find the new barman locking up for the night. When he went to bed he did what was unusual for him. He locked his bedroom door. He had not forgotten the bomb and he was taking no chances.

Chapter 6

SHOCKS

Bertie did not have a very good night, as might have been expected with so much on his mind. He found himself wrestling single-handed with more than one problem. First there was Ginger. Where could he have gone? It was evident that he had still not turned up, or he would have been with Biggles, waiting to be taken to join Algy at the Morven Flying Club. Then there was Biggles. Why hadn't he been at his lodging as he had said he would be? Something must have happened. What *could* have happened? The woman, Mrs Cator, only knew he had gone out. Why had he gone out knowing that he, Bertie, was coming straight back from Polcarron with his pyjamas? There was a mystery about all this and it was no use trying to guess what it was. It could only be solved at Penlock.

So Bertie, turning these things over and over in his mind, had a troubled night. He did manage to get a little sleep eventually, but was glad when the morning came to give him an excuse to get up and complete his toilet ready to move off to Penlock as soon as he could get some breakfast. Only there would he find the answers to the problems that were worrying him. At least, he hoped so.

Some time later, when he opened his door to go down, he became aware of some sort of commotion going on in the hall below. Voices. Strange voices. He went down. To his surprise he found the local

policeman, whom he knew by sight, with a police
sergeant he did not know, engaged in earnest
conversation with the proprietor of the hotel, Mr
Stephen Brunner, who was wearing a dressing-gown
over pyjamas as if he had been brought from his bed.
The new barman, who presumably had unlocked the
front door, was with them.

Having no wish to be involved, Bertie would have
passed on; but the police sergeant stopped him with a
restraining hand. 'Just one moment, sir,' he said. 'Am I
right in thinking you're staying here?'

'That is correct,' Bertie answered.

'Then I take it you knew the barman here; well, the
barman up to yesterday?'

'You mean Tom? I don't know his other name.'

'That's the man I mean,' returned the police officer.
'How well did you know him?'

'Fairly well. That is, as well as one gets to know the
barman of the hotel where one is staying', answered
Bertie, wondering what was coming next.

'When did you last see him?'

'Last night.'

'Where?'

'Outside. Just down the street. He spoke to me. I had
expected to find him serving in the bar, but I was told he
had walked out.' Naturally, Bertie was thinking fast,
trying to keep pace with the questions and the possible
purpose of them.

'Was he sober?'

'Yes, as far as I was in a position to judge.'

'Did he seem quite normal?'

'I suppose I could say that. I noticed nothing unusual
in his behaviour, if that's what you mean. Why? Is
something wrong?'

'Very much wrong,' stated the officer grimly. 'He's dead.'

'*What*!' Bertie stared, aghast. He could hardly believe his ears. 'How did that happen?'

'That's what we're trying to find out,' said the sergeant. 'His body was found early this morning on the beach below the end of the cliff. It looks as if he must have fallen over. We're wondering how it could have happened unless he was drunk; or if it was a case of suicide.'

'He didn't appear to have had too much to drink when he spoke to me,' declared Bertie. 'Nor did he talk like a man contemplating taking his life,' he added, still trying to keep up with a situation that had come as a shock; a severe one.

'What did he speak to you about?' enquired the sergeant, his pencil poised over his notebook.

Bertie was finding this interrogation difficult in front of the hotel proprietor and the new barman. Obviously he would have to be careful what he said. He answered with a reasonable degree of truth. 'I was just driving off in my car to fetch a friend who's staying here with me, when he stopped me to say he'd left the hotel, but was staying on in the village until he could find another job. As I'd always found him a likeable fellow, I asked him if I could help. He said no. In fact, I went as far as to ask him if he was short of money; but he said he could manage.'

'Where did he say he was staying?'

'I didn't pay much attention, but I think he said he'd got a room at number eight, along the front somewhere.'

The sergeant made a note in his book. 'Were you surprised when he told you he'd left the hotel?'

'No.'

'Why not?'

'I already knew that.'

'How did you know?'

Bertie indicated the new barman. 'He told me when I went into the bar. That was the first I knew about it. He said Tom had walked out.'

'Were you surprised?'

'Very much so. I believe Tom had been here for some years.'

'And that's all you can tell me.'

'Yes, sergeant. I think that's all.'

'I see, sir. Sorry to have troubled you. These are just routine inquires, you understand.'

Bertie nodded.

'It's unlikely I shall have to trouble you again, sir, but where shall I be able to find you if I should want you to give evidence at the inquest?'

'I shall be here,' Bertie said. 'Naturally, if there's anything I can do to help. . . .' He was finding this unusual experience of being interrogated by the police somewhat difficult.

'Where are you going now?' asked the sergeant.

'In to have my breakfast. Then I shall be going out in my car. But I shall come back.'

'Very well, sir. That'll be all for now.'

Still shaken by the tragic news he had just heard, Bertie went on to the dining-room and sat at his regular small table for breakfast. He was in a hurry to get away, but he thought he had better have something to eat before he started, in case the day passed without another opportunity presenting itself. What to make of what he had just been told he did not know. Shock had made it difficult for him to think clearly. But of one thing he was in no doubt whatever. Tom had not committed suicide. There had been no hint in his manner, or in what he had said the previous evening, to suggest that he intended taking his life. Nor could he imagine him falling over the cliff by accident. What could he have been doing on top of the cliff, anyway? What, then, was the answer? There appeared to be only one. Murder. Tom had been put out of the way. Silenced. Why? Was it because he knew too much? And let it be known that he knew? Bertie did not forget that someone had seen them together, talking in the car.

He started on his bacon and egg mechanically, without his usual appetite. He was still so engaged when he heard the police depart. Then, to his astonishment, for this had never happened before, into the room came Brunner, still in his dressing-gown, to sit at a small table near him and order a pot of coffee and some toast. It did not take Bertie long to realise the purpose of this. Had Brunner really wanted some coffee he could have had it sent up to his room. No. Brunner wanted to talk; talk to him before he went out. So he was not in the least surprised when Brunner said: 'This is a bad business about poor Tom. He was such a decent chap.'

This, obviously, was an opening gambit to start a conversation.

'Yes,' agreed Bertie. 'It gave me quite a turn.'

'What on earth could have made him do a thing like that?'

'Do what?' asked Bertie, without looking at Brunner.

'Kill himself.'

'We don't know what he did.'

'That's obviously what must have happened.'

Bertie did not answer.

'Don't you think so?' pressed Brunner.

'No, I don't,' Bertie answered bluntly.

'Well, you should know,' continued Brunner, casually. 'You were the last person to see him alive – in your car last night.'

So Brunner knew that Tom had been in his car, thought Bertie.

'What did he talk about?' questioned Brunner.

'Oh, this and that,' replied Bertie, refusing to be drawn. 'He told me about him leaving the hotel, and that he'd be staying on in the village till he could find another job.'

'Why should he tell you that?'

'I wondered that myself.'

'Well, it'll make a lot of difference here.'

'In what way?'

'This new man I've got is only temporary,' Brunner said lugubriously, pouring coffee into his cup. 'He can't stay long, I'm afraid it means that we shan't be able to cater for residents.'

'What exactly does that mean?' queried Bertie.

'I'm sorry, but I shall have to ask you to leave.'

Bertie was not prepared for this. 'But you can't put us out at a moment's notice,' he protested. 'Before we can leave we shall have to find somewhere else to go, and at this time of the year, with the coast swarming with people on holiday, that may not be easy.'

'I didn't mean I expected you to pack up now, this morning,' Brunner said.

'I'm glad to hear that because it would be difficult,' returned Bertie shortly.

'But you see how I'm fixed,' went on Brunner. 'In the circumstances I'd be obliged if you and your friend would vacate your rooms at the earliest possible moment. Why would it be difficult for you to leave right away?'

'Because Mr Bigglesworth isn't here,' Bertie said shortly. 'I shall have to tell him about this. He won't be pleased, you may be sure.'

'Where is he?'

'Staying the night with friends in the country. I'm going to fetch him as soon as I've finished my breakfast.'

'And you'll tell him the position?'

'Of course.'

Brunner finished his coffee and got up. 'Very well. We'll leave it like that. No doubt I shall see you again before you go. I'll have your bill ready by the time you come back. When will that be?'

'When you see me,' answered Bertie curtly.

Brunner left the room.

Bertie did not linger. He felt he was bulging with news and anxious to unload it on Biggles as quickly as possible. Also, he wanted to think, and in the car on the drive to Penlock, he would have an opportunity. So with his brain in top gear, he made his way to the car and set off, confident that he would now find Biggles at his lodging. By this time, too, it seemed more than likely he would find Ginger with him. Things were moving quickly, faster than he alone could cope with them. Clearly, a new plan would have to be made, and only Biggles could do that.

He reached Penlock and pulled up outside Fernside Cottage. He was disappointed not to find Biggles at the gate waiting for him. Possibly with Ginger. But as this was not so, he went to the door and knocked. It was opened by Mrs Cator.

'I've come for Mr Bigglesworth,' Bertie said cheerfully.

'I'm afraid he isn't here,' Mrs Cator said.

'Not here!' Bertie felt as if his legs had been kicked from under him. 'Where is he?'

'I don't know.'

'You're – you're saying he didn't come back here last night?'

'I haven't seen him since he went out last night. He still wasn't in when I went to bed, and this morning when I took him a cup of tea, I found his bed hadn't been slept in.'

For a moment Bertie groped for words. 'I see,' he managed to get out. He smiled bleakly. 'In that case I shall have to find him. Goodbye for the time being.'

Hardly knowing whether he was coming or going, as the saying is, he went back to the car and sank down in the driving seat. This was something he had not reckoned on. What to do about it he did not know, although obviously he would have to do something. He couldn't just sit there all day in the car waiting for things to sort themselves out. He sat deep in thought for some time and then saw a ray of light. Algy. Algy had better know what had happened. At least he would be someone to talk to.

He put the car into gear and set off for Morven Flying Club airfield.

Chapter 7

WHY GINGER WAS LATE

It will be remembered that Ginger was left on the road near Penlock Grange with every intention of walking back to the village, to rejoin the others, as soon as he had made a preliminary survey of the big house.

He could see nothing from where he stood because, as with so many second-class Cornish roads, it was sunk between high grassy banks which completely concealed the view on either side. A profusion of wild flowers sprang from the grass. At the top of the banks were hedges, chiefly a tangle of thorn and briars, with an occasional tree at intervals. Ginger was only interested in one side, the side broken by the entrance to the drive which has been passed on the way to the spot where he now stood: the drive into which the Daimler had presumably turned. It was evident that if he wanted to see anything, there was only one thing to do. Climb to the top of the bank and look over the hedge. If he could not see the house from the top of the bank, he would have to walk back to the drive and do a little cautious scouting from there.

One thing he now noticed for the first time, for he had not been able to see it from in the car, was something in the sky. An anvil-shaped cloud which he knew well enough was almost invariably the forerunner of a thunderstorm. However, that did not worry him. He had been wet before.

With the car already out of sight, he scrambled to the

top of the bank and with some difficulty parted the top
of the hedge sufficiently for him to get a view of what lay
beyond. He was disappointed to find he could not see
very much. In the foreground was a meadow in which
some cattle were grazing, and a few cock pheasants
pecking about here and there. On the far side of the
field, at a distance of about a hundred yards, was a long
wood, or a belt of trees, of mixed timber. At one point,
just showing above the tops of the trees, were two stacks
of chimneys, real or imitation Tudor style. It was plain
they rose from a house of some size, which, Ginger
thought, considering its position in relation to the drive,
could only be The Grange.

He could see nothing else of interest, so all the
information he had gained from his survey was the
precise position of the house. There seemed to be
nobody about. He was not particularly disappointed,
because this was what might have been expected: but
naturally he was not satisfied. He would have liked to
see more. He had learned nothing that was not already
known; so if this was to be the sum total of his
reconnaissance, it seemed as if he had wasted his time.

For a few moments he considered trying to get nearer
to the house; but as he could see no way of doing that
without exposing himself in the open, he did not
entertain the thought. It would be taking an un-
justifiable risk, which he had been ordered not to do.

A footstep on the gravel road made him turn sharply
and he saw he was not alone. Standing looking up at
him was a heavily built man of about fifty years of age
dressed in the manner of a sportsman or a well-to-do
farmer. He carried a twelve-bore gun under his arm. A
dog, a yellow labrador, walked obediently to heel.

The man was smiling in a good-natured way.

'Looking for something?' he enquired pleasantly, in a voice that held just a trace of foreign accent.

Ginger came down the bank. 'Nothing in particular,' he replied. 'I was trying to see where I was. One can't see a thing between these high banks.'

'As I know only too well,' answered the man. As they began walking together down the road he went on: 'Going far?'

'Only as far as Penlock,' returned Ginger casually, seeing no reason to make a secret of it.

As they walked on side by side a pigeon swung into sight overhead. It jinked when it saw them. Up went the gun. *Bang*. Down fluttered the pigeon to hit the road in a cloud of feathers. The dog ran to fetch it.

'Good shot!' exclaimed Ginger. And he meant it. It was a very good shot indeed. A jinking pigeon is never an easy mark.

'These wood pigeons are a confounded nuisance,' said his companion, taking the dead bird from the dog and carrying it by the neck. 'There are too many of them. They play havoc in my vegetable garden. That's why, although the shooting season hasn't started yet, I always carry a gun when I go for a walk.'

'The bird you've just shot isn't a wood pigeon,' Ginger pointed out. 'It's a tame pigeon. It looks like a homer.'

The man looked at the pigeon. 'So it is. At the distance I didn't notice it. Still, what does it matter? Pigeons are all the same as far as I'm concerned. I only had time for a snap shot.' Which of course was true. 'You are a very observant young man,' he concluded, giving Ginger a sidelong glance.

'I know the difference between a wood pigeon and a homing pigeon, although I must admit that in the air I could have made the same mistake.'

At this juncture, as they walked on, from not far away there came a long, low peal of thunder. The man looked up at the sky, now menaced by a dark, fast-moving cloud. 'We'd better hurry or we look like getting wet,' he remarked.

Which again was obviously true.

They quickened their pace, and presently came to the iron gates that marked the entrance to the drive. By this time a few big drops of rain were falling.

'You'd better come home with me till this passes over, or you'll have a wet shirt by the time you get to the village,' the man said.

'I don't think it's going to be much,' answered Ginger, after another glance at the sky.

'Better come in for a bit. There's no sense in getting wet through.'

'Do you live somewhere near?' asked Ginger.

'Only just up here. It isn't far.' The man indicated the drive by which they had paused.

'Is it the house I could see beyond the trees when I was up on the bank?' questioned Ginger, to cover a moment of confusion at this startling piece of information, which came as a mild shock although, as he now realised, he should have suspected it.

'That's it,' said the man. 'Are you coming? If you are, let's get along before the storm really breaks.'

Ginger's first reaction was to decline. It was too much like putting his head in the lion's mouth. The shooting of the pigeon suddenly took on a new significance. Was the incident a demonstration by his companion of how well he could shoot? Then, thinking fast, he realised this might turn out to be a golden opportunity for him to get the information he had been left to obtain. There seemed little risk. After all, he had been invited. It was not as if he had been caught prowling near the house.

With the man waiting, he made up his mind. The chance was too good to let slip. 'This is most awfully kind of you,' he said. 'I will certainly accept your hospitality for a few minutes. As you say, there's no sense in getting wet through if it can be avoided.'

'This way, then.' The man entered the drive and turned to close the iron gates.

This gave Ginger a moment in which to think. His brain was racing in an attempt to keep up with these fast-moving events. First and foremost he was trying to devise a way of letting Biggles know where he was should he be delayed. That was a matter of common sense, for Biggles would certainly come to look for him should he not arrive as arranged. Drop some paper? No, that wouldn't do. He couldn't make the place look as if there had been a paper chase without the man noticing it. He felt in his pockets and found a pocket of book matches. On the flap was an advertisement for the restaurant near to where they lived and at which they often had a meal. They gave the matches away. That would do. He tore off the protecting flap. Biggles would recognise the advertisement, realise only he could have dropped it, and why. At least, he could only hope so. Of course, Biggles might not find it; but if he came looking for him he would almost certainly look at the drive.

He did not drop the flap in one piece. That would be too conspicuous. The man might notice it. Instead, he tore it across, twice. That is in four quarters. He dropped one piece where he stood and the rest at intervals as he joined his companion who, having closed the gates, was moving on. All this had occupied less time than it takes to tell.

Ginger realised he still didn't know the name of the man who had invited him in. He could only guess. He felt it was time he knew. It would be a reasonable question. 'May I ask your name, sir?' he enquired, as they hurried on, for the rain was falling faster.

'Certainly,' answered the man. 'It's Brunner. Julius Brunner. This is my home, Penlock Grange.'

Although by this time Ginger had good reason to suspect this, he felt another twinge of surprise, the reason being that the man beside him did not line up, in his manner or the way he was dressed, with the sort of person he had visualised. He didn't look like a criminal. But that was no criterion. There was another aspect that gave him cause for disquiet. Why, if Brunner was engaged in an illegal enterprise, was he asking him into his house? That was the last thing that could have been expected. Was there a sinister reason for this, or were they all completely mistaken in their suspicions?

However, he had gone too far to withdraw without a reasonable excuse. Rounding the bend in the drive the house came into view. It was larger than he had supposed, being in the manner of an early Victorian mansion house; the sort of house the squire of the village might occupy. As they drew near Ginger saw a face peering at them through one of the ground floor windows. It was a black face, or at least a dark-skinned one. This did nothing to dispel his uneasiness and he made a last attempt to retire. The storm had passed, leaving in its tail only a slight drizzle.

'It's stopped raining,' he observed, coming to a hesitant stop. 'I might as well go on to the village.'

'Having come so far, why not come in and have a cup of tea to give the weather a chance to clear?' replied Brunner smoothly as he opened the front door and entered the hall.

Anything but happy, Ginger followed him in. He couldn't see what else he could do without being pointedly rude, and no one likes to be discourteous in the face of proffered hospitality. He had a feeling that Biggles, who had warned him not to take chances, would disapprove of what he was doing. His qualms were not relieved when a door at the far end of the hall was opened and a man appeared.

Although Ginger had only seen him once, at the village shop, he recognised him immediately. It was the chauffeur of the Daimler. He no longer wore the dark double-breasted uniform with brass buttons, but was dressed in the manner of an indoor servant. A footman perhaps. Was it imagination, Ginger thought, or did the man give him a penetrating stare as he took their hats and hung them on the hall stand? Brunner also handed him his gun. With this the man retired, the dog following him. 'You might bring us some tea,' Brunner said, as the man was leaving them. 'We shall be in the library.'

'Yes, sir.' The man disappeared.

'This way,' Brunner said, putting a hand on Ginger's arm.

They entered a room lined with bookshelves. 'Take a seat and make yourself at home,' continued Brunner easily. They sat in leather covered armchairs facing each other. Not knowing what to say, Ginger waited for Brunner to speak. He did not have long to wait.

'What part of the country do you come from?' was the first and quite natural question.

'From Yorkshire, originally, although I now live in London,' informed Ginger.

'Down here on holiday, I suppose?'

'That's right.'

'Where are you staying?'

'At a little place on the coast some way from here. You may not have heard of it,' answered Ginger evasively.

'And what do you do for a living, if you don't mind me asking?'

'I fly aeroplanes,' answered Ginger truthfully, seeing no reason to lie.

'Really! How interesting. I've often wished I'd learned to fly, when I was younger. Now I'm afraid I'm past it and have to be content with pursuits more in accord with a man of my age.'

'And what may they be?' queried Ginger, really for something to say.

'I like sailing. I also do a little shooting in the season. That's really why I live here. I raise a few pheasants. From your remark when I pulled down that pigeon, I gather you've done some shooting, too.'

'When I get the opportunity, which isn't often,' Ginger said.

'You must come here and have a day with me when we start on the pheasants,' suggested Brunner.

'That's very kind of you. I'd like to,' accepted Ginger.

At this moment the door was opened and a coloured man carrying a tray came in. Ginger thought it was the same man he had seen at the window as they approached the house, but he couldn't be sure of that. The man pulled forward a small table and put the tea tray on it. 'Mr Bates would like a word with you, sir, when you can spare a moment,' he said, and then retired.

'Excuse me a minute,' Brunner said to Ginger as he got up. 'Something always seems to be going wrong in a

house of this size. I'd better see what the trouble is now.
I shan't keep you long. Help yourself to tea.'

He went out, leaving Ginger a prey to fresh doubts
and misgivings, although up to now the conversation
had been perfectly normal and Brunner's behaviour
had been all that could be desired. What, wondered
Ginger, did the man Bates want to see him about so
urgently? Bates. Who was Bates? Was he the servant
who had met them in the hall? The chauffeur? Then he
remembered. Bates was the name of the man he had
picked up on the radio, at the aerodrome, when he was
trying to make contact with Biggles. 'Pug' Bates he had
announced himself when he sent out a warning signal.
Was this a coincidence. Ginger didn't know what to
make of it.

He had not long to reflect. Brunner came back,
resumed his seat and pulled the tea tray towards him.
His manner was unchanged, Ginger was relieved to
note.

'Why, you haven't poured yourself any tea,' chided
Brunner. 'Never mind. Sit still. I'll give you a cup. Do
you take sugar?'

'One lump, please.'

'There you are.' So saying, Brunner filled Ginger's
cup and handed it to him.

'Thank you,' Ginger said. 'There's no need for you to
wait on me.'

'Ah, but there is,' answered Brunner. 'You're my
guest, don't forget.'

As Ginger sipped his tea Brunner went on, still in a
matter-of-fact one of voice: 'My chauffeur, Bates, tells
me he saw you in the village earlier this afternoon.'

Ginger realised he was getting on dangerous ground,
but it would be foolish to deny it. 'If he was in the village

he might well have done so, as I was there,' he admitted.

'What were you doing in the village?'

'I was in a car with some friends. One of them wanted some cigarettes, so we stopped at the shop,' explained Ginger. Again he drank some tea to prepare himself for more difficult questions which he felt sure would be forthcoming. He was finding it a little difficult to think clearly.

'I believe your friend is named Bigglesworth,' Brunner said evenly. His voice sounded far away.

'Yes, that's right,' Ginger agreed.

'He's staying at Polcarron, I think.'

'Yes, that's right,' Ginger said again, unable to think of anything else to say.

'What's he doing in this part of the world?' questioned Brunner.

Ginger struggled to think of a non-committal answer. So Brunner had known all the time, he thought, or else Bates had just tipped him off.

'Answer me,' rapped out Brunner. His voice now had a hard quality.

Ginger was finding it difficult to think at all. His brain seemed to have stopped working. He drank some more tea, but his hand was so shaking that he spilt more than he swallowed. He opened his mouth, but no words came. The room was beginning to spin, the face in front of him, now enormous, spinning with it. Then, suddenly, the truth struck him like a blow on the head from a hammer. My goodness! he thought desperately. I've been doped.

The last thing he remembered was the crash of his cup and saucer as they fell on the floor and shattered to pieces.

Chapter 8

PROBLEMS

When Biggles had told Mrs Cator, at his lodging at Fernside Cottage, that he was going to take a short walk for some fresh air before turning in, he meant exactly that. It was too early to go to bed, and in any case he had to wait for Bertie to bring his things from Polcarron. He was worried by the long absence of Ginger and did not feel inclined to sit in the cottage parlour listening to Mrs Cator talking of matters that were of no interest to him. He wanted to do some uninterrupted thinking, and the best place for that was on the quiet country road.

It was hard to see how any harm could have come to Ginger provided he had obeyed orders, but it was perhaps natural that when he went out he should turn in the direction of the Grange, or the drive that led to the house; for this was near where he had left Ginger, so he would be bound to see him should he be making a belated return to the village.

It was a fair night with a clear sky and the moon nearly full, so he strolled on, deep in thought, pondering the situation. He saw no one. Not a soul. Not even a late vehicle; and in due course found himself at the iron gates at the entrance to the drive leading to the house of the man in whom he now had an interest. Mr Julius Brunner. Naturally, he stopped. The gates were shut. He tried them and ascertained they were not locked. He rested against them, peering between the bars up the moonlit drive, wondering if Ginger could have been so foolish as to risk using the drive. It seemed most unlikely. He could not see far up the drive, first because of the elbow bend in it, and again because it was accompanied on the right-hand side by a hedge of evergreen shrubs, laurels, rhododendrons, or something of that sort. The other side was a plain open meadow. So much Biggles could see. He had no intention of making a closer inspection, seeing no purpose in it. That would be better done in daylight, if it had to be done at all. So there he stood, thinking, satisfied that from whichever way Ginger might come, down the lane or up the drive, he would be there to intercept him. He stood there for some time, content to be doing nothing. Everything was dead still. Occasionally some of the usual night sounds came from a distance. The bark of a dog. The lowing of a cow. The cry of a night bird. The whistle of a distant train.

After a while he found himself staring at a small spot on the ground just inside the gates. It shone white in the light of the moon. Actually, he was looking at it for some time without being aware of it. Then, suddenly, he became conscious of it and he wondered what it could be. It was not a pebble. Had somebody dropped something? A silver coin, perhaps. That was what it looked like. He was still not particularly interested, and being disinclined to move, he continued to gaze at the object. Then he noticed a second white spot close to the first. This was too much. His curiosity had to be satisfied.

Quietly, not allowing the iron latch to rattle, he opened one of the gates and walked through. Stooping, he picked up the object of his attention, to find that, after all, it was only a tiny piece of paper. Or to be precise, pasteboard. He nearly screwed it up there and then and put it in his pocket to dispose of later, thinking some litter-bug had passed that way. On second thoughts, still more from curiosity than any real interest, he looked at it closely. There seemed to be some sort of mark on it; printing. The moon did not give sufficient light for him to read it, so still actuated by curiosity he flicked on his petrol lighter. For a moment he gazed uncomprehending; then, realising what it was he held in his hand, his muscles went taut. It was the name of a small restaurant close to his flat in London. One he often used. The one they all sometimes used.

There could be only one answer as to how it came to be there. A piece torn from a packet of book matches. Only Ginger could have dropped it. The chances of anyone in the locality using the restaurant were too remote to be entertained seriously. Two strides and he had picked up the second piece. In doing this he saw two more pieces. He picked them up and put them together in the palm of his left hand. They fitted exactly. The slip of cardboard, with the name of the restaurant, was complete. It was the flap of a packet of book matches.

With his brain now active, Biggles went back through the gate and closed it behind him. This, he decided, was no accident. Nobody except Ginger could have had such a packet of matches; and he could not imagine Ginger wantonly tearing up the flap and making a litter at the entrance to a private drive for no reason at all. Even if he had used the last match, he would not have done that, detesting, as he had often said, people who make a mess of the countryside. No. This had been deliberate. He had torn off the flap of a book of matches, and tearing it into quarters thrown the pieces on the ground. Why? It did not take Biggles a minute to work it out. There could be only one reason and it was obvious. Knowing the pieces, if they were found, would be recognised, he had left a mark to show he had gone up the drive. Should he be prevented from returning, it would be an indication of where he was. But why had he gone up the drive? That was a question not so easily answered. In fact, it was beyond Biggles' imagination. He could hardly be expected to visualise the events that had occurred on the spot where he now stood.

Why had Ginger taken such a precaution? He must have known that in going up the drive he would be taking a risk. There must have been more to it than that. Had he been afraid that he might not be allowed to return? That suggested he had been forced to do what he had done. It seemed that his fears had been justified. He had not returned. Had he done so, he would have picked up the litter he had dropped, if for no other reason than the tell-tale mark was no longer required. It followed, therefore, he was still somewhere up the drive, in the grounds if not actually in the house. The reason why he had not joined the others in the village was now explained.

Biggles perceived he was now in a difficult position; one that called for serious thought. First and foremost was the clear indication that Ginger was in danger. This was the dominating thought in Biggles' head as he sat on the bank and considered what he should do about it. He saw there was more than one course open to him. He could do nothing at all; just sit at the gate to await Ginger's return. If he did return. He might not, in which case valuable time would have been wasted. Even if he did appear, it might not be for some considerable time, in which case there was Bertie to consider. He would be completely in the dark, not knowing what to do when he returned to the village and failed to find him.

Another course, Biggles pondered, would be for him to go back to the village to await Bertie's return, when he would tell him what he had discovered. They could then take some action together. There would be difficulties about that, though. What could they do with the car? There was no garage in the village. Bertie had no lodging, so where could he spend the night? Sitting in the car? That did not seem a satisfactory arrangement, and in any case it would serve no useful purpose. They couldn't leave the car standing on the road without anyone in it. The battery might run out, leaving the car without light, when it would be a danger to anyone else on the road.

The truth is, for once Biggles did not know what to do for the best. In the meantime, if nothing was done, Ginger might be in mortal danger and any delay might be fatal.

There was one other course open. It was perhaps the obvious one. He, Biggles, could go up the drive alone hoping to find Ginger, or some clue that would solve the mystery of his disappearance. Reveal where he had gone. There might, Biggles thought in a fever of apprehension, be time for him to do that and get back to the village to catch Bertie when he returned from Polcarron with his pyjamas. He would be some time yet, for not only was there the journey each way, but there would be a delay while he collected the toilet things he had gone to fetch. The snag here was, should he return to Penlock and fail to find Biggles at his lodging, he would be at a loss to know what to do.

Biggles realised there seemed to be an argument against whatever he did; but he felt it was time he was doing something. He went back to the gates and looked up the drive. There appeared to be no difficulty in getting to within sight of the house on account of the evergreen hedge that ran parallel with the drive. This would provide cover for a cautious approach. He made up his mind suddenly. He would do some preliminary exploring, anyway, if nothing more. Near the house he might see something, somebody, that would give him an idea of what had become of Ginger. Bertie would have to wait. He did not lose sight of the possibility that, if Ginger had fallen into a trap, he might make the same blunder.

Opening the gates quietly and closing them behind him, he moved on to the hedge, prepared to dodge into it should anyone appear from either direction. There was enough moonlight to give him warning of that. The air was still, with no wind to drown the sound of footsteps or an approaching car. He had not forgotten that the Daimler lived here and it might be on the move.

He made good progress, and rounding the bend in the drive came to within sight of the house. It was not as far as he had supposed; but it was larger. Not that he could see much of it. All he could really see was its bulk silhouetted against the night sky. He could, however, just make out the front door, or the porch that protected it. This, he noted, was supported by columns up which some sort of creeper had been trained.

Chinks of artificial light at the edges of blinds or curtains showed that four rooms were at present occupied, and he paused to consider them. There were two on the ground floor, a large room and one he took, from a fanlight over the front door, to be the hall. A light showed on the first floor, presumably an upstair sitting-room or more probably a bedroom. There was another light higher up that could have come from an attic, perhaps a servant's bedroom.

He continued to advance, slowly, until he was brought to a halt by the fact that the hedge along which he had been moving came to an end; or rather, it straggled out into what appeared to be a rose bed. He could see some flowers showing faintly white in the light of the moon. Here the gravel drive swung round past the entrance porch in a way that would enable a car, calling at the front door, to leave without having to reverse. This of course was a common arrangement with large houses.

Biggles stopped. There seemed to be nothing more he could do short of going boldly to the door to ask if Ginger was there, a procedure which he thought would not serve any useful purpose, particularly if Ginger was being detained against his will; and he could not imagine him staying there for so long for any other reason.

He waited, listening intently. No sound came from the house. He looked around. He could see no one. There seemed no reason why he shouldn't go nearer, close enough to hear movements, or voices, inside the house. He crossed the open drive swiftly and took up a position close to the outside wall of the porch, which was as near as he dare go without taking an unwarranted risk. Hardly had he reached his immediate objective than there came a sound that sent him ducking into the corner where the wall of the porch joined the house. The creeper on the pillar, which he had previously noted, turned out to be a climbing rose, as he discovered painfully from the usual thorns.

However, it provided a certain amount of cover.

The noise that had alarmed him was that of a car coming up the drive. For a moment he thought it might be Bertie, coming brazenly to look for him; but this notion was soon dispelled. The headlights of the car came round the bend, for a few seconds lighting up the lower part of the house. Biggles bowed his head to conceal his face as the glare of light swept across him. One thing was already evident. From the speed at which the car was travelling the newcomer was no stranger. It came to a dry skid. The driver got out. Risking a peep Biggles saw he was alone. The man advanced quickly to the door and rang the bell. The door was opened. Biggles heard the new arrival say: 'Good evening, Bates. Is my brother in?' He could not see the man, but he recognised the voice. It was Stephen Brunner, the landlord of The Fishermen's Arms at Polcarron. So the two men, Stephen and Julius, *were* brothers, he noted.

'Yes, I'll tell him you're here,' replied Bates. And again Biggles recognised the voice. Bates was the chauffeur, the man who drove the Daimler.

Chapter 9

A LONG WAIT

There was a brief interval of silence broken only by the sound of retreating footsteps; then Biggles, crouching uncomfortably in his corner behind the rose bush, caught the aroma of cigar smoke and guessed another person had arrived on the scene; the caller's brother, presumably. Julius Brunner. The first words he spoke practically confirmed this.

'Hello, Stephen. What brings you here at this hour?' said the voice from the house. 'I was just thinking of running over to see you. I have a bit of a problem on my hands.'

'So have I,' returned Stephen, harshly.

'Oh! What's the trouble?'

'I have reason to think those two men staying with me at Polcarron are police spies,' stated Stephen. 'I thought you had better know about it. We shall have to do something.'

'All right,' replied Julius shortly. 'There's no need to panic. We should be able to deal with them. But there's no reason to stand talking here. Come in.'

For a moment Biggles thought this was to be the end of a conversation which he found exceedingly interesting. But to his satisfaction Stephen replied: 'No, I won't come in. I'm in a hurry to get back. I have things to do. What's *your* problem?'

Julius answered. 'These two men you've had staying

with you. I think there are more than two. There's
another. I've got him inside.'

'What! How did that happen?'

'I was walking down the road and caught him spying
on the house. Anyhow, that was what it looked like. So I
brought him in. He didn't give any trouble. Why did
you have to come here? If you wanted advice what was
wrong with using the telephone?'

'Not with those cops about. It isn't safe. I don't know
where they are at the moment, but when they come in
I'll tell them their rooms have been let, so they'll have to
get out.'

'Is that wise? It might be better to keep them under
your nose where you can see what they get up to.'

'I've seen enough. They've been talking to my
barman. He's been with us too long. He may have
noticed something, so I've sacked him. He's been with
one of them tonight. I'd like to know what they were
talking about. But never mind about that. I'll see to it
he doesn't do any more blabbing.'

'Your trouble, Stephen, as I've told you before, is
you're frightened of your own shadow,' said Julius,
critically. 'Just go on behaving normally.'

'If I were you I'd get rid of everybody,' said Stephen.
'This house might be raided any day. How many clients
have you got here?'

'Only two. They're all set to go. In fact, you might
take them with you and drop them off at Portwin Cove
where they'll be all ready to go across in the morning.'

'Not me. I'm not going to Portwin Cove tonight. I've
got other things to do.'

'All right. I'll send Bates over with them. Then
they'll be all ready for a day's fishing tomorrow.'

'Where will you put them?'

'The usual place, till I'm ready to take them across to the island. They can wait there. They'll be safe enough.'

'I wouldn't bother with them; it's too risky with these coppers about. I'd turn 'em loose, now, let 'em go where the hell they like.'

'They'd take a poor view of that,' returned Julius. 'Don't forget they've each paid five hundred pounds for their tickets. No, we can't let 'em down at this stage. Word would get round that we weren't to be trusted and that would ruin the whole business. We'd never get another customer, and I have in view one or two that should be little gold mines.'

'I still don't think this strip of coast is safe any longer,' muttered Stephen.

'Don't worry. They should know me well enough by now, and the boat,' answered Julius easily.

'What are you going to do with the cop you're holding here? Are you sure he's a cop and not just a stray hiker?'

'Bates saw him this afternoon in the village with one of the two men you've got staying at your place – what's his name – Biggleswick, or something like that. So he must be one of the party. I fancy he was left to keep an eye on the house.'

'What are you going to do with him?'

'Let him go.'

'You must be mad.'

'He doesn't know what happened to him. I'll tell him he had an accident, or a heart attack, and was brought here to be taken care of.'

'I'd silence him for good. He might talk.'

'He can talk as much as he likes. He doesn't know anything that matters. You may be sure I took good care of that.'

'I'd make certain he couldn't talk,' Stephen said curtly.

'That'd be a crazy thing to do,' argued Julius. 'It would start something. If the police planted him here, should he disappear, they'd never rest till they found him. And suspicion would fall on this house. Don't you see, by letting him go, it would give the impression that we've nothing to hide; nothing to be afraid of.'

'All right. You please yourself, but I know what I'd do,' retorted Stephen, grimly. 'Now I'll be getting along to make sure everything is okay at my end.'

'I'll have anyone here who matters out of the house by the morning,' promised Julius.

Here the conversation ended abruptly. Stephen Brunner returned to his car. He slammed the door; he started the engine: the lights came on and he drove off. The front door of the house was closed. Footsteps retreated down the hall and silence returned to Penlock Grange.

Relieved, Biggles stretched his cramped limbs and removed a trailing rose briar from the back of his neck. With what profound interest he had listened to the enlightening conversation between the Brunners can be imagined. He waited for a minute or two to make quite sure that the coast was clear, and then made his way to the hedge by the drive to think things over. And he had plenty to think about; so much that his brain was racing as it strove to put the information he had just overheard into its proper perspective. He looked at his watch and observed it was now after midnight.

He found a convenient spot at the bend of the hedge from which he would be able to watch the front of the house and digest what he had heard and what he should do for the best. His first inclination was to hurry on in the hope of finding Bertie still waiting for him, so that he could tell him what he had learned, after which they could perhaps act together. It would obviously be unwise to keep such important information to himself in case he should run into trouble. The others should know as soon as possible what he now knew: that the two Brunner brothers were definitely engaged in some illegal traffic.

Then he thought of Ginger who was somewhere in the house and decided that he must come first. From what Julius had said he did not think he was in any immediate peril. What if Julius changed his mind in view of the sinister suggestion his brother had made about Ginger's final disposal? Julius had said he intended to let him go, telling him he had met with an accident. That could only be taken to mean that Ginger had been hurt. How? How serious was his injury? That was the point. Biggles concluded it couldn't be very bad, or Julius would not have talked about turning him loose.

Another factor had to be taken into account. One of paramount importance. He, that is, Biggles, and Bertie, were known for what they were. Police officers. They were to be turned out of The Fisherman's Arms. When?

At this stage of his cogitations Biggles became aware of activity near the house. The Daimler has been brought round. It had stopped by the front door. The driver, presumably the man named Bates, got out, went into the hall, presently to emerge carrying two light suitcases and accompanied by two other men. Biggles worked it out that Julius was doing what he had said he would do; clearing the house of 'clients' in case the police made a swoop. The two men were being taken to

Portwin Cove, wherever that might be, to be ready for a day's fishing. In other words they were to be transported overseas.

With the 'clients' in the car, the chauffeur took his place at the wheel and the Daimler moved off up the drive. Seeing it coming. Biggles crouched back to watch it go past. He could not see much. The vague figure of the driver in front and the two passengers in the back seat. He would have liked to follow it to its destination, but as that was not possible he dismissed the matter from his mind and returned to thoughts of Ginger, with whom he was more concerned. He had not been in the car, so apparently he was still in the house.

Julius had said he would let him go rather than have the police make a search for him. When would he do that? No time had been mentioned. If Julius kept his word, there was no need to worry. In due course Ginger would appear in the village. What disturbed Biggles was the possibility that Julius, influenced by his brother, might have second thoughts about letting him go. Stephen had hinted darkly at disposing of the prisoner altogether. That could only mean murder. Would they go as far as that?

Torn by indecision, Biggles stood staring at the house, knowing that if anything happened to Ginger, now that he knew definitely he was in the house, he would never forgive himself if he failed to make an effort to rescue him. On the other hand, if Ginger was to be released, there was no need for him to do anything. He had only to wait for him to appear. To try to break into the house might well make matters worse.

In this critical crisis it took Biggles some time to make up his mind, but finally he reached a decision. He resolved to remain where he was and keep the house

under observation until Ginger walked out, or was
carried out, whichever it was to be. If he did this, he
assured himself, it would be impossible for Ginger to
leave the house without him being aware of it.

Thrusting a way well into the hedge, but with the
front of the house still in view, he settled down to wait.
He glanced up at the moon. It was over its zenith, but
would still last for some time.

An hour passed. Nothing of importance happened.
One by one the lights in the house went out until only
the one on the top floor remained. Another hour
dragged on. Biggles found this waiting a weary
business. Fortunately the night was not cold, or the
tedium would have been worse. He never took his eyes
off the house, not daring to relax his vigilance for a
minute.

It was about four in the morning when he heard the
Daimler coming back. At least, he assumed it to be the
Daimler, and presently saw that he was right. He
watched it go past. The driver was now alone,
apparently having left his pasengers at the place
arranged. The Daimler did not stop at the front door,
but went on to the back of the house, presumably to its
garage. Biggles had thought it might now take Ginger
somewhere, but evidently this was not the intention.

As the time dragged on Biggles found it increasingly
difficult to keep his eyes open, wherefore he was
thankful when the grey ghost of another day crept up
over the horizon. Now, in daylight, he thought, his task
would be easier. But he still had to wait. In fact, it was
nearly eight o'clock when the front door of the house
was opened and, to Biggles' intense relief, Ginger
appeared. For a minute he stood on the threshold
talking to someone inside. Then, with a parting wave,

which struck Biggles as odd, he started walking up the drive, obviously unhurt.

Biggles did not move. He waited until Ginger was level with him and then said quietly: 'I'm here. Keep walking. I'll stay on the other side of the hedge and meet you at the gates. I don't want to be seen from the house.

Ginger faltered for a moment from the shock of hearing Biggles' voice, but continued walking until they met at the gates.

'Am I glad to see you!' greeted Ginger.

'I can believe that,' Biggles answered.

'What were you doing?'

'Waiting for you, of course. What else would I be doing here at this hour of the morning?'

'How did you know I was in the house?'

'A little bird told me,' replied Biggles. 'But never mind you asking me questions. You've got a bit of explaining to do. We'd better not stand here. We can talk on the way to the village. Are you all right? I mean, not hurt, or anything?'

'There's nothing wrong with me except a splitting headache,' returned Ginger.

They started walking towards the village.

'They told me I'd had a heart attack,' went on Ginger.

'Who told you?'

'Julius Brunner.'

'Did you have a heart attack?'

Ginger's lip curled. 'Not on your nellie. I'm not that dumb. I was doped.'

'How did that happen? What were you doing in the house, anyway? Tell me about it. This whole business has got me foxed.'

Ginger answered. 'What happened when you left me

on the road was really very simple. A man came along. He seemed a very nice fellow. He had a dog with him and carried a gun. I took him to be a farmer or a sportsman. As we walked down the road together it started to rain. He invited me to take shelter in his house until the storm had passed over. Naturally I accepted. It wasn't until we were through the gates that I realised that we were going to Penlock Grange and the man beside me was Julius Brunner. Thinking I might learn something I carried on. From what happened after that I realise he must have been suspicious of me all the time. He gave me tea. What was in it I don't know, but it did something to me. He asked questions and I had to answer. I couldn't help myself. Then I passed out and must have been out for some time. When I came round I was lying on a bed feeling pretty seedy. Brunner was there. He told me I'd had a heart attack. He gave me some medicine and I felt better. He asked me what I wanted to do, which surprised me. I said I'd push on home right away. He saw me off, all very nice and affable.'

'You were lucky you didn't fall into the hands of his brother, Stephen, who keeps our pub at Polcarron,' Biggles said. 'He's a nasty piece of work. He'd have bumped you off. I heard him tell Julius so. You say Julius asked you questions. What questions?'

'I can't remember,' Ginger had to admit. 'I was already under the influence of the dope he gave me.'

'No matter. I can guess. I learned quite a lot myself last night. I can't blame you for what happened.'

'How did you know I was at the Grange?'

'I found the clue you left at the gates.'

'Oh yes. Of course. The book of matches. I'd forgotten about that. By the way, where's Bertie?'

'I don't know. I didn't go back to the village last night. He was to fetch my small kit. He must be wondering what the devil has happened. I'm hoping we shall find him waiting in the village.'

It so happened that they did not have to go as far as the village. Before they reached it they saw the car coming towards them. Bertie was driving and Algy was with him.

Bertie pulled up and jumped out. 'Here, I say, what the blazes have you been playing at?' he demanded hotly.

'I haven't been playing,' returned Biggles evenly. 'I've been working. Don't argue now. Get back in the car and drive us somewhere where we can talk. I've got news for you.'

'*You've* got news!' exclaimed Bertie. 'Wait till you've heard mine.'

They all got in the car. 'Where to?' asked Bertie.

'Anywhere, as long as it's well clear of Penlock,' answered Biggles shortly. 'It isn't a healthy spot for us at the moment.' Bertie drove on.

Chapter 10

ACTION IS PLANNED

Bertie drove the car some distance from the village until, coming to a lay-by in the usual high banks to allow vehicles to pass, Biggles ordered him to stop. 'This'll do,' he said. 'Now we can talk. It's time we compared notes. Bertie, you go first. What's your news? Make it short because things are moving fast and we've no time to lose.'

'Right you are. Fasten your safety belt, old boy, because you're going to need it,' began Bertie.

'Get on with it, you're wasting time,' Biggles said curtly.

'Okay – okay. Don't rush me,' complained Bertie. 'I'll start from where I left you last night to fetch your pyjamas so that you could spend the night at Penlock. When I got to our pub in Polcarron I found that Tom the barman was no longer there. There was a new man behind the bar. He told me Tom had walked out. That was a lie. He was sacked at a moment's notice.'

'How do you know that?'

'He told me so himself. He stopped me when I was on my way back to Penlock with your kit. When I got to Penlock you weren't there. I waited for hours. You didn't show up. What could I do?'

'What *did* you do?'

'I parked the haversack at your lodging and went back to The Fishermen's Arms for the night. I didn't feel like sitting in the bally car all night, in the village, where I might have been spotted by somebody from the Grange. This morning I got up early feeling sure I'd find you at Fernside Cottage. When I went down to snatch a bite of breakfast there was a rumpus going on in the hall. It was the police.'

'What police?'

'The local lads, of course.'

'It'll complicate things if they're going to barge in. What did they want?'

'They were asking questions about Tom.'

'What had he done?'

'Nothing. He couldn't do anything. He was dead.'

Biggles stared. '*Dead*!'

'His body had been found on the beach at the foot of the cliff.'

'Are you saying he'd killed himself?'

'No. I don't believe that. He was as right as rain when he'd spoken to me a few hours earlier. He told me he'd been sacked, so he'd taken a room in the village until he could get another job. He said he'd been sacked because there was something crooked going on at the pub and he'd tried to find out what it was. It looks to me as if they weren't satisfied with sacking him, but they bumped him off to prevent him doing any more talking.'

'Talking to whom?'

'To me, perhaps. I know someone was watching us when we were talking in the car.'

'So you think he was murdered?'

'I'm convinced of it. He didn't talk to me like a man who was contemplating suicide. He was cold sober, so I don't see how it could have been an accident. He left me to go to his new quarters, nowhere near the cliff.'

Biggles was silent for a moment, his lips in a hard line. 'The murdering hounds,' he breathed. 'Now we shall *have* to get them.'

'The police were making inquiries. They think it must have been an accident, or suicide as a result of losing his job. They questioned everyone, including me.'

'How much did you tell them.'

'As little as possible for the time being. Having no sort of proof, I didn't say I thought he'd been murdered. That would have started something. I would have had to tell the lot, who we were and why we were there.'

'You did the right thing.'

'Jolly good. When the police had gone, and I was having a cup of coffee, Brunner came into the dining-room and he too started asking me questions, to find out, I think, what I really thought about this business. I let him think I was inclined to accept the suicide theory. I fancy he's suspicious of us. Anyway, he says he's let our rooms, so we have to get out.'

'We'll see about that,' muttered Biggles cogently.

Bertie went on: 'When I got to Penlock this morning and found you hadn't been home all night, I got really worried. Not knowing what else to do, I dashed over to the airfield to put Algy wise as to what had happened. Wait a minute. I haven't finished yet. As I was bringing Algy here to help me to look for you we met that perishing Daimler. We decided to follow it to see what it was up to. We ended up in a little place on the coast called —'

'Portwin Cove,' put in Biggles.

Bertie's eyes opened wide. 'How the devil did you know?'

Biggles smiled faintly. 'Let's say I'm clairvoyant. I've been busy, too. Carry on. What happened at Portwin Cove?'

Algy came in. 'I left Bertie with the car and did a spot of scouting on foot. The Daimler stopped as near as it could get to the little harbour. Three men got out and went to a boat moored alongside the quay. One of them whistled. A man appeared, a caretaker, I suppose, from below deck. Two of the new arrivals joined the fellow on the boat and they disappeared below. The driver of the Daimler went back to his car and drove off. I shadowed it to Penlock Grange. That's all.'

'This boat?' queried Biggles. 'What sort was it?'

'I'd call a cabin cruiser. Pretty robust-looking craft. Looked as if it was built for salt water. Sleep four, for a guess.'

'You didn't get its name?'

'No. I daren't go too close. I didn't want to be caught spying.'

Biggles nodded. 'Fair enough. Now I'd better put you right in the picture by telling you what happened to Ginger yesterday and to me last night.' He went on to relate the story of what had happened at Penlock Grange, which included the conversation he had overheard at the porch.

When he had finished Bertie said: 'So that's how things stand at present. What's the drill now, old boy?'

'It isn't easy,' Biggles replied thoughtfully. 'We now have a pretty good picture of what the Brunners are doing. They must be making a thousand quid a trip in this racket. What we haven't got is evidence that would stand up in court. We've no proof that these men now in the boat are being taken abroad. Even if we had a boat, which we haven't, it would obviously be a waste of time to follow them when they leave, because we'd be spotted.'

'Why not nail these two men who we know are on the

boat at the moment?' suggested Algy.

'What could we charge them with? Shark-fishing? That's what they'd say they were here for. It might even be true. There's no law against that.'

'They might be a brace of crooks on the run, if you see what I mean,' offered Bertie.

'And they might not,' returned Biggles. 'Then what? No, that won't do. The risk is too big. We should have shown our hand for nothing. Besides, the boat might already have left. Let's try to get the whole thing in perspective. The racket, as I see it, is this. The two men now on the boat will go out ostensibly shark-fishing. I'd wager there's fishing tackle on the boat in case any questions are asked. A coastguard might see the boat leave. He'd have no reason to stop it. No doubt he knows it by sight. So the boat goes. Somewhere, well clear of land, the two men on board with be switched for two other men, presumably illegal immigrants. They are probably waiting at this moment to be picked up. The coastguard sees the boat come back with the same number of men on board as when it went out, so he does nothing about it. Why should he? It may well be that the two men who come ashore will be wearing the clothes of the men who went out. What we don't know is where these unwanted immigrants are waiting. They could be on another boat; a French fishing boat, for instance. On the other hand they might be waiting on some island.'

'Why an island?' questioned Ginger.

'Because last night something was said about an island. It could be anywhere. This country is surrounded by islands. It would hardly be the Isle of Man. That's too far away. And I think we can rule out the Isle of Wight as being too near home. From what part of the Continent are the people waiting to come here mostly likely to come?'

'France,' guessed Ginger. 'It's the nearest point. Don't forget the boat at Portwin Cove is supposed to be for shark-fishing, so it wouldn't do for it to be away too long.'

'I'd say you're right,' agreed Biggles. 'Let's say it's France. How are we going to confirm it?'

'What's wrong with doing a little spotting from the air?' suggested Algy. 'It's time we were doing something or we shall miss the boat – literally.'

'Would you recognise the boat if you saw it at sea?'

'I think so, although I wouldn't swear to it. If I saw a cabin cruiser well out to sea on a course for the French coast, it'd be a clue.'

'Okay,' Biggles said briskly. 'Let's get on with it. I'll take you to the airfield. When you get off the ground head for Portwin Cove and check if the boat you saw last night is still in the same place. If it is, watch it. If it's gone, try to pick it up in the Channel and mark where it makes its landfall. Keep well clear, or it may be realised what you're doing. You may need help, so you'd better take Ginger with you. If you learn anything important, you should be able to contact me in the car by radio.' So saying Biggles started the car and took the road to Morven aerodrome.

'What are *you* going to do?' asked Algy, as Biggles drove on.

'When I've dropped you and Ginger at the airfield, I shall go to Penlock, collect my kid from Mrs Cator and apologise for not turning up last night. There's no point in staying in the village now Brunner knows about us. Then I shall go on to Polcarron. Bertie and I will have to find somewhere to hang up our hats for the night, so it might as well be The Fishermen's Arms. Our suitcases are there, anyway.'

'You haven't forgotten we've been kicked out?' reminded Bertie.

'We'll see about that,' replied Biggles in a hard voice. 'A hotel can't do that sort of thing and I shall tell Brunner so in no uncertain terms. We've a good reason for staying on. The police might wish to question you again about Tom, particularly if there's to be an inquest. You might have to give evidence. It'd look suspicious if you weren't to be found. It'd look as if you'd bolted. Strictly speaking, now there's suspected murder on the book we should go to the local police officer in charge and tell all we know; but we can't do that without upsetting our apple-cart. It'll have to wait. We shall have to explain our behaviour later on, of course.'

Within half an hour the plan of action had been carried as far as it could go. That is, Algy and Ginger went off in the aircraft. Biggles and Bertie, having watched them go, set off for Penlock village to collect Biggles' kit from Fernside Cottage. As a result of this diversion it was nearly midday by the time they finally reached Polcarron. As they cruised down the single street to the hotel, they were stopped by the local policeman who stepped in front of the car with a hand raised.

Biggles wound down his window. 'What's the trouble, officer?'

'I've been looking for you, sir. At the hotel they told me you were leaving,' informed the constable.

'Nothing of the sort,' Biggles answered. 'We're on our way there now. Did you want something?'

The policeman was looking at Bertie. 'It's about the inquest on Tom Draper who was barman at the hotel.

As it seems you were the last person to see him alive, we may have to call on you to give evidence.'

'When is the inquest?' inquired Bertie.

'The day after tomorrow. Eleven o'clock at the church hall,' was the answer.

'Okay. Let me know. I shall be about; probably at the hotel,' advised Bertie.

The policeman saluted and stepped back.

Biggles drove on and pulled up at the kerb outside the hotel. They went in. In the hall they were met by the proprietor.

'Come to collect your things, I hope,' he said brusquely.

'We've come to do nothing of the sort,' replied Biggles coldly. 'We've come because we're staying here, and here we intend to stay.'

'But you can't do that,' protested Brunner. 'I've let your rooms.'

'Then you'd better unlet them again,' Biggles said succinctly. 'We're staying. And, moreoever, we shall expect proper service. So see to it.

'I'll call the police,' threatened Brunner.

'I wouldn't advise you to do that. Think again.'

'You can't tell me what I can do,' stormed Brunner.

'That's where you're wrong,' stated Biggles. He took a pace nearer to Brunner and looked him straight in the eyes. 'Let me tell you this,' he went on frostily. 'If you don't already know it we have some powerful friends, and if I have any more trouble with you I'll have your licence withdrawn. Think that over and stop throwing your weight about with me. Apart from anything else we're under police instructions to remain here in order to be on hand, if required, to give evidence at the inquest in two days' time on your late barman. We know why he left here and our story may not be the same as yours.'

Brunner did not answer.

'We shall be down for lunch in five minutes,' concluded Biggles, and followed by Bertie passed on.

They went up to their rooms. At the top of the stairs Bertie faced Biggles with a doubtful expression. 'Here, I say, old boy, you piled it on pretty thick. Why tell him as much as you did?'

'I told him nothing he didn't know or suspect,' returned Biggles. 'It sometimes pays to carry a war into enemy country. Anyhow, I'm not going to be given the run-around by that cheap little grafter.'

'He could do us a mischief – if you see what I mean,' Bertie said dubiously.

'No doubt he'd like to, but with the police in the offing I don't think he'll try anything like that. Two more sudden deaths in the village would be too much of a coincidence. When we've had a wash we'll go down to lunch. Then we'd better take turns to stand by the car in case Algy tries to get us on the radio. See you downstairs in five minutes.'

Chapter 11

ALGY REPORTS

Biggles and Bertie met downstairs in the dining-room for lunch as arranged. Brunner was not there, but, somewhat to their surprise, the usual waitress appeared to take their order. The first course, soup, was brought and served. Bertie had his first spoonful half-way to his mouth when Biggles rapped out: 'Hold it.'

Bertie, his eyes questioning, lowered his spoon slowly back to the plate. 'What's wrong, old boy?'

'Maybe nothing – but. Hasn't it struck you that the soup looks a bit oily on top?'

'I hadn't noticed it.'

'Moreover, it seems to have a peculiar smell about it.' So saying Biggles lifted his plate and sniffed.

Bertie did the same thing. 'Now you mention it, yes, you're right,' he agreed. 'Seems sort of familiar, some-how – if you see what I mean.'

'It should be,' Biggles said meaningly.

Bertie sniffed again. 'I seem to know it, but I can't place it.'

'I can,' returned Biggles. 'There's one aroma I shall never forget as long as I live. One whiff of it and I'm back in the old days when they were flying Pups and Camels.'

'Are you talking about castor oil?' Bertie said, suddenly understanding.

'That's what it smells like to me. I used to stink of the

stuff myself when I was flying Camels.* The left
shoulder of my tunic was black with the oil chucked
back by the engine. That was because, like a lot of
pilots, I always flew with my left elbow resting on the
side of the cockpit, so that I could get a clear view in
front.'

'What's the idea?' Bertie said. 'It must have got in by
accident.'

'Not likely. What would castor oil be doing in the
kitchen?'

'But why? It wouldn't poison us.'

'No, but it could put us out of action for a while.'

The waitress came back to collect the plates. She
looked surprised to see the soup untouched.

Biggles asked her: 'Who made this soup?'

'Mr Brunner,' she answered.

'Where is he now?'

'In the kitchen.'

'Go and tell him I want to see him.'

The girl went off. In a minute Brunner came into the
room. 'Something wrong?' he queried sourly.

'Yes. We don't like your soup,' Biggles stated coldly.

'What's the matter with it?'

'You put too much castor oil in it. It stinks. I
understand you made it.'

'Nonsense. That's impossible,' blurted Brunner.

---

*The rotary engines of the early days of flying were lubricated
with vegetable oil, normally castor oil, which, being used by the
gallon, made them expensive to run. The oil went straight through
the cylinders and was flung out of the cylinder heads. Being hot it
gave off a sweet, sickly smell which, once experienced, was
unmistakable. One could usually tell a Camel pilot by the black oil
stain on his tunic.

'Have a taste of it,' invited Biggles. 'Take my spoon. I haven't used it.'

'I've just had my lunch.'

'I'll bet you have,' sneered Biggles.

'But how could castor oil have got into the soup?'

'It got in because you put it in, and I can guess why,' rasped Biggles. 'If I had the time I'd pour this lot down your throat. See that it doesn't happen again or I'll fetch the police to have a look at things here. That's all. Now let's have something to eat that hasn't been decorated.'

Brunner glared, but said nothing. He went out.

Bertie said to Biggles. 'You know, old boy, somehow this seems to have taken the edge off my appetite. From now on I shan't fancy the grub here. There's a little fish bar along the street. How about walking along and knocking back a dish of chips?'

'No thanks. Not while I'm paying to be fed here. That little rat isn't going to chase me off the premises. I don't think he'll try any more tricks like that now I've threatened to bring in the police.'

They continued their meal, cold roast beef and boiled potatoes, in silence. As far as it was possible to judge there was nothing wrong. When they had finished they went out to the car and moved it to its old place on the quay. Having settled in this position, Bertie put on the headphones and prepared to explore the air for possible signals, first, of course, trying their own wave-length.

'I see my old gossip making for the seat; I'll go and have a natter with him, or he may think I've gone all hoity-toity,' remarked Biggles. 'Let me know if anything comes through.'

'Just a minute,' Bertie said tersely. 'I believe this is Ginger.'

Biggles waited.

'Okay, Ginger, come in,' Bertie said, speaking to the instrument. 'Bertie here. Yes, Biggles is with me. Over.' A pause, and Bertie went on. 'Sorry, but we've been grabbing a spot of lunch. Go ahead. I'm listening. Over.' There was another pause, a longer one this time, while Bertie listened. Finally he said: 'Roger. We'll be there. Right away. Over and out.' He switched off and turned to Biggles, who was waiting impatiently for the news.

'What was all that about?' enquired Biggles.

'They picked up the boat this morning, a long way out, and shadowed it. They know where it landed the two passengers and think it's now on its way home with only a two-man crew on board. It's on a course for this part of the coast, but they can't say exactly where. They reckon it should be in in about an hour.'

'Are they going to follow it in?'

'No.'

'Why not?'

'They say there's no point in it. There are no fresh passengers on board. It's more important that they should see you at once to give you the news. It would take too long on the radio. They're heading flat out for the aerodrome and reckon to touch down in less than half an hour. They want you to meet them there. Ginger sounded peeved because we didn't answer the signals earlier. Says he's been trying on and off to get us for the last half-hour.'

'We can't be in two places at once,' Biggles said. 'Okay. Let's get weaving for the airfield.'

Without any more ado they set off, and travelling fast came in sight of the aerodrome just in time to see the Auster come in. Parking the car they hurried to meet the occupants.

'Where the devil have you been?' demanded Algy irritably. 'We've been trying to get you all morning. This is urgent.'

'Then get on with it and don't waste time grousing. We've been busy, too,' retorted Biggles. 'Where did the boat unload the two passengers?'

'You're not going to believe this,' stated Algy.

'Give me a chance. Where was it?'

'The Channel Islands.'

'Which one?'

'I don't know which one.'

Biggles frowned. 'What do you mean – you don't know which one?'

'How could I be expected to know? Have you any idea of how many there are?'

'Frankly, no. I've only heard of four.'

'There are scores. In fact, there seemed to be hundreds. The Channel is littered with islands.'*

'You're joking.'

'Would I joke at a time like this? All I know is they landed on one of the smaller islands. I marked it well, so I hope I can find it again.'

'I take it the island is one of ours?'

'I wouldn't know about that. Why? Don't they *all* belong to us?'

'I'm not sure about it myself, but I have a vague idea that some, those nearest to the French coast, belong to France. We shall have to find out about that.*

---

*Ask any schoolboy to name the Channel Islands and he will probably answer without hesitation, Jersey, Guernsey, Alderney and Sark. A boy who has studied his atlas might add Herm and Jethou. But it is unlikely that he would be able to name the many others, such as Lithou, Burhou, Ortae, the Casquets, Les Ecrehou

'You'd better tell me exactly what happened this morning,' requested Biggles.

'We were a long time finding the boat and I'm only surprised that we found it at all,' began Algy. 'It was a long way further out than I had imagined and, thinking of petrol, I was about to pack it in when I spotted it in the distance, still going like stink judging from the wake it was leaving behind it. I don't know what sort of boat this is, but you can take it from me it's no ordinary craft. It must have a thousand horses in its engine. I'd say it was knocking up something like forty knots.'

'Are you sure this wasn't a destroyer?' put in Biggles, dubiously.

'Quite sure. I know a destroyer when I see one. It was the only small craft in view, anyway, so I couldn't have been mistaken.'

'Okay. Carry on.'

'Remembering you had overheard some talk of an island, I worked it out that its course was set for

or the Chausey Islands, a group that lies close to the French coast and incidentally, belongs to France. In fact, there are a great many islands, large and small, within the region embraced by the Channel Islands. Nobody seems to know exactly how many there are. Some are mere heaps of rock, most of which are now uninhabited, although ruins of houses show they were once occupied. One or two are privately owned. One is a nature sanctuary. On one a man lives alone, making a living by lobster fishing, his catch being collected from time to time by a boat from one of the larger islands.

The islands were once described as 'pieces of France dropped in the Channel and picked up by England'. Actually, a thousand years ago they were part of the Duchy of Normandy, and when William the Conqueror, Duke of Normandy, captured England, he brought them with him – so to speak. In the circumstances, therefore, Algy's apparently poor geography becomes understandable and excusable.

Guernsey,' continued Algy. 'I was wrong. It kept well clear of Guernsey. You can always recognise Guernsey because half the island is covered by glass; greenhouses where they grow early tomatoes and what have you. So I thought it must be Jersey the boat was making for. Nothing like it. Again it kept clear. By this time, with islands on all sides, I was getting a bit dizzy . . didn't know what to think.'

'You had a map,' Biggles pointed out.

'A fat lot of use that was,' snorted Algy. 'It only shows the main islands. What I needed was an Admiralty chart. But let me finish. Getting worried about petrol, because there was still no sign of this daft business coming to an end, I was on the point of turning for home when the boat suddenly changed course and shot into a little cove on one of the smaller islands. That was it. I couldn't see much, because I daren't go close for fear of someone guessing what I was doing. They must have seen me, anyhow. I reckoned that didn't matter much, because I wasn't the only plane in the air. There were two or three other small machines about, trips, I imagined, between the islands, or from the main islands to the French mainland.'

'What happened on the island, that's what I want to know?' asked Biggles.

'The boat didn't stay five minutes. I could see some sort of building, or maybe a tent, with two men standing in front of it. They hurried down to the boat. There was a short discussion. The two men on board joined the others on the shore and the boat pushed off, again at top speed, leaving all four men on the island. I kept the boat in sight till I was sure it was heading for home, then I made flat out for here. Why the boat has to travel at such a heck of a lick I don't know.'

'I can tell you,' Biggles said. 'It had a long way to go. If it's apparent excuse was shark-fishing, it wouldn't do for it to be out too long — certainly not overnight.'

'Yes, I suppose that's the answer,' agreed Algy. 'I didn't think of it. I worked it out like this,' he went on. 'I fancy the original intention had been to dump the two men on the island and bring back those already there, but for some reason there had been a change of plan; as if Brunner, or whoever was in charge of the boat, had got the wind up about something.'

'You're probably right,' Biggles replied. 'Things have been moving fast here. It's known the police are on the job, and I know for a fact that the trip today was to get rid of two men Brunner had staying with him at Penlock Grange. How far away was the boat when you last saw it?'

'Some distance. Oh, and I'd better tell you this. Once it nearly stopped and the men still on board seemed to be fishing.'

Biggles nodded. 'To bring a fish home would prove it had been fishing and account for it being out for so long,' he said dryly.

Bertie came on. 'So what's your next move, old boy? Get airborne and have a dekko at this island Algy's been talking about; that's if he can recognise it again?'

'I could do that,' declared Algy. 'There's no question of landing on it, if that's what you have in mind. It's only about three hundred yards long and less than half that wide; and it's all rocks.'

'In that case we'd better forget about it for the moment,' decided Biggles. 'If it isn't too late, I'd like to see where the boat lands, who comes ashore and where they go.'

'How are you going to do that?'

'It might just be possible. This is how. Listen carefully. This is important.' Biggles spoke swiftly. 'I shall head for the coast in the car with Bertie. Algy, take Ginger, get topsides, and try to pinpoint the boat if it's still at sea. You might just be in time to spot it before it comes in. We can keep in touch by radio. Don't forget to top up your tanks before you start. You'll still get to the coast before us. If you can find the boat, what I want to know is where it appears to be making for. If I know that I'll get to the place to see what happens – who comes ashore and where they go.'

'What if it's already in harbour?' asked Algy.

'Unless you're able to recognise it you might as well forget it. The plan flops.'

'Where exactly will you make for when you leave here?'

'Polcarron.'

'Why there?'

'It's as handy as anywhere. It'll do for a start. We shall have to eat and sleep somewhere and it might as well be The Fishermen's Arms. Bertie will have to be in Polcarron anyway, for the inquest on Tom Draper. The police want him handy. As soon as you've finished what you're going to do, Algy, go straight to London and tell the Air Commodore how things stand – the boat, the island, Penlock Grange – the lot. You can tell the story as well as I can. Ask him what he wants us to do. This thing's getting a bit too big for us to handle alone. Then you'd better come back here. Got that?'

'I get it. Where shall I find you?'

'Try the pub at Polcarron. Right! Let's get cracking. We haven't too much time. Keep in touch. We shall be listening for a signal.'

'Okay.'

In five minutes, leaving Algy and Ginger preparing to refuel the Auster, Biggles and Bertie were in the car on the road to Polcarron.

Chapter 12

BACK TO POLCARRON

Before reaching the coast, and still four or five miles from Polcarron, Biggles and Bertie saw the Auster race over them; whereupon, as soon as it was judged the aircraft was in sight of the sea, as Biggles was at the wheel Bertie tuned in for signals. 'Now we should soon know what the luck's like,' he remarked cheerfully.

The luck appeared to be good, for they had not long to wait before the first message came through. 'They've found her,' Bertie told Biggles crisply. Presently he went on: 'She's still six or seven miles out, travelling in top gear and seems to be on a course for Polcarron. Algy says he's keeping well clear but won't lose sight of them.'

'Fine. That suits us,' Biggles said, accelerating. 'We should just beat them to it.'

A few minutes later, with the sea in view, Ginger came in, and again Bertie reported to Biggles. 'Yes. Unless the boat changes course at the last minute it's going to be Polcarron. The boys want to know if they're to stand by or carry on with the operation as arranged?'

'Tell them we'll take over now. We should be able to see the boat ourselves in a couple of minutes. They can press on for London.'

Bertie transmitted the message. 'Okay, me lucky lads. Off to town you go. That's all. Over and out.' He switched off.

Within five minutes they were running into

Polcarron. 'There she is,' observed Bertie. 'Just coming in. We've got her on the dot. So what next?'

Biggles slowed the car to a crawl. When it was level with the little harbour he let it run to a stop. 'It looks as if she intends to tie up against that little concrete mole,' he said quickly. He looked around. 'There doesn't seem to be anyone about except my old gossip Sam, on the seat. I'll tell you what, Bertie. You get out and walk along to see what they do next. It doesn't matter if they see you. They'll take you for a casual visitor.'

'What about you?'

'I'll stay here in the car. If Bates is about – the fellow who drives the Daimler, he'll recognise my old Ford. Not that it matters. He once spoke to us here, you remember. You walk along to see what they do and where they go.'

'Okay, old boy.' Bertie got out and strolled along the quay, deserted except for old Sam on his usual seat.

Biggles kept his eyes chiefly on the boat, now alongside the mole that formed a protecting wall on the far side of the harbour. But he noticed that when Bertie was level with the seat Sam got up and walked along with him; for what purpose of course he did not know unless it was mere idle curiosity.

Watching the boat Biggles saw two men doing something on the forward deck, but was unable to see what it was. They then walked together along the mole towards the village street, at the end of which they went up a flight of steps and out of sight. Bertie and Sam walked along the mole as far as the boat, stood talking for a minute and then walked back and up to the street where they, too, could no longer be seen. A minute or two passed; then Biggles saw Bertie coming along the quay alone, towards the car.

'Well?' queried Biggles, when he arrived. 'Where did they go?'

'They've gone into The Fishermen's Arms.'

'The devil they have.'

'The Daimler is in the car park.'

'Who were the two men? Did you recognise them?'

'One of them. Bates, the chauffeur. I've never seen the other, but I have a feeling it might be Julius Brunner, brother of the fellow who keeps the pub. Old Sam thought that was who he was, having seen him in the village once or twice. He told me something else, although I don't know quite what to make of it. You saw us walk along to the boat?'

'They were doing something with a shark. Not a very big one. It's still lying on the forward deck.'

'So they must have managed to get one, Algy, or Ginger, said he thought he saw someone fishing.'

'No. That's the point. They didn't catch one.'

'I don't get it.'

'According to old Sam that fish has been dead for a week. He says he's seen it before, once if not twice. Matter of fact that was why he went along, to have a look at it. He swears it's the same fish he saw one day last week. It's a blue shark. They don't come close inshore. According to Sam you have to go at least twenty miles out to get 'em.'

'Well, he should know.'

'He can't make out what those two fishermen are up to.'

'I can understand that,' Biggles said.

'What do *you* think is the idea?'

'There's one obvious answer to that. A dead shark provides proof that the boat has been out fishing – should anyone in authority come along to make a check.'

'So that's it.'

'I can't think of any other reason and I'm not going to waste time now trying to think of one.'

'What are we going to do?'

'We might as well go along to The Fishermen's Arms and have something to eat.'

For a moment Bertie looked startled. 'You're not forgetting who's already in there?'

Biggles smiled. 'That's one of the reasons why I'm going in. We may learn something. I'll take the car up and park it outside. We're at a loose end, anyhow, until we get word from the Air Commodore what he wants us to do. Things have reached the stage when I don't feel like acting on my own responsibility.' He started the car and moved off.

'You know, old boy, there's one thing about all this that puzzles me; it doesn't seem to add up,' Bertie said thoughtfully. 'You said that when you got suspicious of this sharking set-up, you noticed that the number of men who came back was the same as the number that went out. Which meant that any Customs official who happened to be about would take no notice.'

'That's right,' agreed Biggles.

'Yet today four men went out, but only two came back. Surely that meant taking a chance of being asked what happened to the two passengers?'

'No. You've overlooked a point of detail.'

'What have I overlooked?'

'The boat didn't return to the harbour from which it set out. It left from Portwin Cove, but came back to Polcarron. It's most unlikely, therefore, that anyone who saw it depart would see it return; so no questions would be asked. I fancy that's a regular practice which has enabled them to get away with what they're doing.'

'Pick up the customers at one place and come ashore again somewhere else.'

'Exactly.'

Bertie frowned. 'How is it you always manage to come back with the bally answer?'

Biggles smiled. 'It's just a matter of using the grey stuff you have between the ears. I had to develop the habit when I was young. Here we are.' He brought the car to a halt outside the front entrance of The Fishermen's Arms. 'As we shall need the car again presently we'll leave it here.'

'And what exactly are you hoping to do now, if I may ask?'

'Before I do anything else I'm going to have a drink,' declared Biggles. 'I'm no camel. I need sustenance from time to time. The only thing that has touched my lips today has been a thin slice of cold beef. We'll call at the bar on the way to the dining-room. I'll stand you a noggin. What's it to be?'

'A glass of beer, thank you kindly.'

Pushing open the swing doors they entered the bar to find it empty except for the new barman.

'Two half-pints, please,' ordered Biggles.

The barman looked at him but did not move.

Biggles repeated the order.

Still the barman looked. He did not move or speak.

For a moment, naturally, Biggles looked puzzled. 'You suddenly struck hard of hearing?' he enquired.

'I heard you,' the barman said.

'Then how about doing something about it?'

'I've had orders not to serve you.'

'Oh! So that's it. Who gave the order?'

'The boss.'

'Is he in?'

'I think so.'

'You'd better find out. You can either produce the beers I ordered or go tell him I'm sending for the police; and I don't think he'd like that. We're not drunk, so you've no excuse for not serving us. These are licensed premises and this is a public bar. Now jump to it.'

After a moment's hesitation the barman disappeared through a door at the end of the bar.

'What an infernal cheek,' growled Bertie, polishing his monocle with his handkerchief.

'Not to worry,' returned Biggles cheerfully. 'He'll serve us.'

The barman came back. Without a word he took two glasses from the shelf behind him, filled them and banged them on the bar so that some of the beer was spilt.

'Top them up and then wipe the glasses,' ordered Biggles in a voice that would have cut iron. 'I want to put the beer down my throat, not over my collar.'

The barman obeyed.

'That's better,' Biggles said.

'That'll be two shillings,' snapped the barman.

Biggles paid the money. 'You can now go and tell your boss that when we've drunk this we're going through for a meal.'

'Lunch is off.'

'Then someone had better put it on again or you're likely to lose your catering licence.' Biggles did not raise his voice.

Again the barman went off. He returned with the boss, Stephen Brunner, who said, curtly: 'You're late.'

'I know, and I'm sorry; but we were delayed by circumstances beyond our control,' explained Biggles, evenly. 'But remember, we are residents, so let's not have any argument about it. We need something to eat and we're having it here. Some cold meat and pickles will do us.'

'The police were here a little while ago asking for you,' informed Brunner in a surly voice. 'I'm to tell you that the inquest on my late barman has been postponed.' Brunner spoke as if he was reluctant to pass on the information yet dare not withhold it.

'Indeed! Why postpone it?'

'How should I know?'

'Well, I suppose they have their reason,' Biggles said. 'It sounds as if they might suspect foul play. That settles any question about us leaving, doesn't it? I mean, as there's nowhere else in the village we shall have to remain here, whether you like it or not.'

'I'm not sure about that,' growled Brunner.

'I am,' returned Biggles smoothly. 'I'd advise you not to go out of your way to look for trouble. Come on, Bertie.' With that he walked past Brunner and on into the dining-room.

They found two men there, at a table with food in front of them. They were Julius Brunner and his chauffeur Bates. They stopped eating to stare, apparently unprepared for the encounter.

'Nice day for a spot of angling,' Biggles called cheerfully to Julius Brunner. 'Have any luck today?'

'We caught a fish,' was the answer, in a curious voice.

'Only one? Somebody told me you usually came back with a brace,' returned Biggles easily.

'Who told you that?'

'A friend of mine. Tell me something, if I'm not being too inquisitive. When you catch a shark what do you do with it?'

'It goes to the fishmonger for cats' meat.'

Biggles smiled. 'I couldn't think of a better way of disposing of it.'

These pleasantries were brought to a close by the entrance of Stephen Brunner carrying a tray. He brought it to the table where Biggles and Bertie were sitting and served them with what Biggles had ordered.

'That suit you?' he questioned gruffly.

'Just the job,' acknowledged Biggles. 'Sorry if I've disturbed your little party.'

'Don't mention it,' muttered Stephen Brunner with unconcealed sarcasm. Then he added venomously, as if no longer able to control his temper: 'You think you're smart but I'll get even with you one of these days.' With that he joined his brother at the other table.

'No threats, now,' chided Biggles reprovingly, and then proceeded calmly with his meal.

'What's the idea of this back-chat?' Bertie asked softly.

'There's nothing like getting the enemy rattled; it interferes with his judgement,' answered Biggles.

The meal proceeded without further conversation. When it was finished Biggles sat back with a sigh of contentment. 'That's better,' he remarked, looking at his watch. 'Now, as there's nothing we can do here we might as well be getting back to the airfield to see if the boys are there with orders from headquarters. Let's go,' he concluded, getting up.

'We shall be back,' he called across to Stephen Brunner as they went out.

'You're asking for trouble,' remarked Bertie when they were outside.

'It's sometimes the quickest way to bring matters to a

head,' Biggles answered soberly, as he started the engine.

Chapter 13

BIGGLES SHOWS HIS HAND

Biggles and Bertie arrived at the airfield to find the Auster already there, on the small concrete apron, with Algy and Ginger standing by it apparently waiting for them.

'Come on – come on,' grumbled Algy. 'You've been a long time getting here.'

'We've had things to do,' Biggles explained.

'Such as?'

'Among other things, arguing the toss with Brunner about staying on at the pub.'

'Well?'

'We're staying. He can't put us out. The inquest on Tom Draper has been postponed and the police may want Bertie to give evidence.'

'I know. The Chief may have been indirectly responsible for that. He got in touch with the Chief Constable of the County and suggested a postponement. It would allow time for a post mortem examination of the body to ascertain if Tom had been drinking.'

'I'll swear he was cold sober when he spoke to me,' put in Bertie. 'He told me he was on his way to his new lodging for the night.'

'Never mind about that,' came back Biggles impatiently. 'What does the Chief suggest we do about all this?'

'You can ask him yourself. He's here.'

'Where?'

'In the clubhouse, waiting for you.'

'How did that happen?'

'I flew him down. When I had given him the gen he decided he'd have to see you, and to bring him down here would be quicker than fetching you to London. We collected the Chief Constable on the way, as we're operating in his territory. They're together now, inside, talking things over.'

Biggles whistled softly. 'By gosh! We have got things buzzing.'

'There's a reason. Listen to this. I haven't finished yet. That crook Limpy Logan, who you saw come ashore when you were last staying in Polcarron, has been picked up in London. He's squealed, and is ready to turn Queen's Evidence. As a result there wasn't much I could tell the Air Commodore.'

'So he knows the name of the island where the switches are made.'

'No. There's a snag about that. Logan doesn't know the name of the island. He was never told. But from our description, and going over the chart with the Air Commodore, we think it must be one of a group of islets called the Petit Caraloes. The trouble is, they don't look the same two days running, or even at the same time of day. It seems there's a big rise and fall of the tide in the Channel Islands. According to Admiralty Sailing Directions, the islands I saw might be little more than a reef at high tide. The tide was out when I saw it, so it would look bigger than it really is.'

'What has the Chief decided to do about it?'

'I don't think he's made up his mind yet. There are difficulties whichever way the job's tackled. You can ask him yourself. Here he comes, now.'

Biggles turned and saw Air Commodore Raymond coming towards them accompanied by a man he did not know. Both were in civilian clothes.

The Air Commodore came up. 'Good work, Bigglesworth,' he greeted. 'You've proved what you suspected was going on.' He introduced his companion as Colonel Hudson, Assistant Chief Constable of the County.

'Thank you, sir,' acknowledged Biggles. 'We should be about ready to get the case buttoned up.'

The Air Commodore looked dubious. 'It isn't as easy as that. The thing still bristles with difficulties. Before we strike we've got to get unshakable evidence. Remember, Julius Brunner is a rich man, so you may be sure he'll employ the best lawyers in the country for his defence. After all, the charge may be one of murder. Do you know where he is now?'

'An hour ago he was at Polcarron, in The Fishermen's Arms, talking with his brother Stephen. If Julius has left, he has probably gone home to his place at Penlock. He can't know how much we know, so he could be picked up there for questioning, if not actually charged with smuggling human freight. So where's the difficulty?'

The Chief Constable answered. 'It's this island rendezvous. We want to know who's there and exactly what's been going on. We don't want to step on the toes of the Channel Island authorities; or France, if it comes to that. We must know who this island belongs to. As I understand the position there's no place for a plane to land, so the only way of getting to it would be by boat.'

'It wouldn't need a battleship,' Biggles said. 'A coastguard cutter could do the job. I could go with it to watch things from our angle.'

The Air Commodore looked at the Chief Constable.

'How does that strike you?'

'I suppose it could be done that way – if we knew the exact position of the island,' was the thoughtful answer.

'Then all that remains is to get organised,' Biggles said cheerfully. 'When we've cleaned up this little island nest of crooks we can tackle Penlock Grange and The Fishermen's Arms. May I suggest that for a start we go to Polcarron to check what's going on there?'

'What exactly have you in mind?' questioned the Air Commodore.

Biggles continued. 'I see it like this, sir. We know two men were left on the island. With the weather fair an attempt may be made to take them off. I'm pretty sure Julius Brunner would be in favour of that, to keep faith with his customers, who had paid for their passage. Stephen would probably be in favour of leaving them there. The boat should tell us what is happening. It was tied up at Polcarron. If it's no longer there, it may have gone to the island. Then there's their car, a Daimler. If it's no longer at Polcarron, we can assume it has taken Julius home to Penlock. We shall learn nothing here, so I'd suggest we move on to Polcarron. I have a car here.'

'You still haven't answered the big question,' put in the Chief Constable. 'Let us suppose the boat has gone, is already out at sea? Then what? How are we going to locate this island?'

'I can't see any great difficulty about that,' answered Biggles. 'We have an aircraft. You lay on a boat and we'll handle the aviation side.'

'How exactly?'

'If the boat has left Polcarron, the plane should be able to spot it and shadow it. When the boat lands at the island, all the plane has to do is circle over it. That should show the coastguard cutter exactly where it is.

But all this depends on the state of affairs at Polcarron, so I'd suggest we go there without losing any more time.'

After a brief conference this was agreed by the two senior officers. Biggles' last words to Algy were: 'There's nothing you can do for the moment except wait here with Ginger and stand by for signals. That won't be until we find out what the position is in Polcarron. Then I'll call you. If the boat is still there it's a washout. If it's gone your job will be to find it; that, of course, is assuming the Chief Constable can get some sort of official craft to follow it – under your direction of course.'

The Chief Constable put in a word. 'It's no use me trying to fix anything until we know for certain that the boat has put to sea.'

'That's understood, sir.'

'I'll get on the telephone from somewhere as soon as we know if we shall have to make this a marine operation.'

'I'd suggest either the police station or post office at Polcarron would be the best place,' offered Biggles.

Nothing more was said. With four on board the car set off, Algy and Ginger standing by the Auster. Little was said on the journey, all there was to say having already been said, and in due course the car was cruising up the sea road at Polcarron. Biggles brought it slowly to a stop against the kerb. His eyes surveyed the little harbour. The boat they sought had gone.

'So now we know,' he murmured. 'The question is, where has it gone? To the island, or has it simply moved to another berth? I see an old friend of mine on the beach. He may have seen which way it went. I'll ask him. The Daimler is still outside the pub, so it looks as if

Julius Brunner is still here. If his chauffeur has gone with the boat, he may be waiting for him to come back. He may not be able to drive the car himself.'

The Air Commodore spoke. 'You'd better call the plane and get it started on the search.'

'Before I do that I'll have a word with Sam, my friend on the bench,' Biggles answered. 'He should know which way the boat went when it left here. There's no point in starting to search the Channel if the boat has only moved along the coast. I shan't keep you a minute.' Biggles got out, and without any apparent haste, in case he was being watched from The Fishermen's Arms, made his way to the beach where old Sam Pretty was basking in the sun, wearing his usual navy blue guernsey and peaked cap.

'Hello there,' greeted the old seaman, in his rich Cornish burr, as he joined him. 'Ain't seen you lately. Thought you musta' left for good.'

'Oh, I've been about,' returned Biggles casually, as he sat down.

'What about Tom Draper dying sudden like he did?' said Sam. 'That was a bit of a shock. Couldn't believe it when they told me.'

'Yes,' agreed Biggles. 'What do you make of it?'

'Can't make nothin' of it. Seems mighty queer to me. He didn't look the sort of chap to pop off like that.'

'They reckon it was an accident,' prompted Biggles, to get the old man's opinion.

Shaking his head Sam gave Biggles a sidelong glance. 'That warn't no accident.'

'What makes you say that?'

'Tom wasn't alone on the cliff path that night.'

'How do you know?'

'I've got eyes. I seen another man there, walking

behind him.'

'Who was it?'

'Couldn't say. It was dark.'

'Have you told the police this?'

'No.'

'Why not?'

'Nobody's arst me, I told you there was more going on here than meets the eye. I reckon there still is. Strangers a' comin' and goin'.'

'What strangers?'

'How should I know? It ain't none o' my business.'

Biggles changed the subject. 'That shark-fishing outfit was here not long ago. I see it's gone. Another fishing trip, I suppose.'

'Could be – could be. If it is they won't do no good today. They ought to know that.

'Why no good?'

'The tide's set wrong. Change o' wind. Water's too cold.'

'Did you see the boat leave?'

'Couldn't help but see it. I was sittin' here.'

'How long ago was that?'

'Couple of hours, mebbe.'

'Who did it take?'

'Brunner what owns the pub, the fellar who drives that big car standing outside now and a coupla strangers like I spoke about. They arrived in a hell of a hurry, it seemed to me, for a quiet day's fishing. Came up the street so fast in one of these little red racing cars they might have killed someone. Two young men went in. Went into the pub. Had some luggage with 'em. Presently one of 'em comes out and puts the car into one of the pub's lock-up garages, so it looked like they was goin' to stay. After a while they came out with Stephen

Brunner and that chauffeur and they all go down to the boat. The strangers still had their luggage, which struck me as queer.'

'Why?'

'It didn't look like fishing tackle to me. I couldn't work that out, not nohow, when they cast off.'

'Which way did the boat go?'

Sam pointed straight out to sea. 'That was the way they went, and that was the way they were still going, full speed ahead, when I last saw 'em.'

This was all Biggles really wanted to know. He didn't stop to wonder who the two strangers might be. Already he had been longer than he had intended, so excusing himself he returned to the car to find the others listening to the one o'clock news.

'I should really be getting back to London,' the Air Commodore said, frowning.

'Why? What's happened?' inquired Biggles.

'There's been another big bank raid. I should be on the spot to deal with it. Usual business. The get-away car was a red Jaguar. Stolen, of course. Shouldn't take us long to find it.'

'Did you say a *red* Jaguar?' queried Biggles, tersely.

'That's what they say. Why?'

'A red sports car arrived here, apparently in a devil of a hurry, about two hours ago. Two men in it, with luggage. According to my information the car is now in one of the private lock-up garages of The Fishermen's Arms. The two men who came in it, and their luggage, are now in the boat, which has put to sea, apparently on a fishing trip. What do you make of that? Is it coincidence – or is it?'

The Air Commodore was staring hard at Biggles' face. 'You don't think . . . ?'

'It's a possibility. Why not? The raiders would be anxious to get out of the country as quickly as possible, and if they knew about the racket that's been going on under cover of this shark-fishing, they might well have made for here. In fact, the whole thing might have been arranged beforehand.'

'We'd better have a look at this car,' declared the Air Commodore, starting up from his seat.

'You won't find the loot in it even if it turns out to be the get-away car.'

'Why not?'

'If I'm guessing right it's in the luggage that was put on the boat. The car won't tell us anything, so there's no hurry in dealing with it. It'll still be here tomorrow, and probably for a long time after that, since no crook will want to be seen with a vehicle which half the police in the country must now be looking for. I think it would be better to concentrate on the boat. I'll call my boys on the radio and tell them to get weaving. Not that there's any hurry about that, either. If the boat's bound for the island, it'll take it the best part of the day to get there.' Biggles turned to the Chief Constable. 'If I may presume to suggest it, sir, if it could be arranged, this is where you might lay on one of your official boats with two or three sturdy fellows on board in case of trouble.'

'Why not wait here and arrest the whole gang when they come ashore?'

'We don't know for certain that the boat will come back here; or, if it does, some of the passengers might have been put ashore somewhere else. Moreover, it's unlikely that the two new men who went out with the boat will come back in it.'

'That's true,' agreed the Chief Constable. 'The most likely place to get what we want is Falmouth. It isn't far away. They might let us have a coastguard patrol boat, with its crew.'

'If they can do that it might come here to pick up anyone who wants to go with it. The skipper will need someone to tell him exactly what we're trying to do.'

'I'll get on the phone right away,' said the Chief Constable.

Biggles turned to the Air Commodore. 'As this looks like being a long job, sir, don't you think it would be a good idea to grab something to eat while we have the opportunity?'

'Eat? Where?'

'At The Fishermen's Arms. There's nowhere else. It might be worth having a look to see what's going on there, anyway.'

'You can go if you like; I'm not particularly hungry,' replied the Air Commodore. 'My mind is too taken up with this business.'

'As we look like having a long trip in front of us, I'd feel happier with a few sandwiches in my pocket, if nothing else,' Biggles said. 'An old soldier always has an eye on his rations.'

This being settled, what was in fact the second part of the scheme was put into operation. The Chief Constable went off to the post office to telephone, and Biggles got busy making contact with Algy at the airfield. Having succeeded in this, he gave his orders in detail, telling him exactly what he wanted him to do.

By the time he had finished the Chief Constable was back. 'That's all right,' he stated. 'A coastguard cutter is on the way. It should be here in about half an hour.'

'Fine,' said Biggles. 'While we're waiting I can slip along to the pub for a few sandwiches as an excuse to see what goes on there. I'll bring some for you Bertie. While

I'm away stand by the radio in case Algy comes through.'

So saying, Biggles left the car and walked briskly down the pavement to The Fishermen's Arms. Pushing through the swing doors he looked into the bar in passing. There were no customers; only the barman, polishing some glasses, who gave him a curious look.

Biggles did not stop but went on to the dining-room. There was only one person there, too, Julius Brunner, apparently having his lunch. On Biggles' entry he looked at him with his fork raised. 'So you've come back,' he said shortly. 'What do you want now?'

'Some food, what else?' answered Biggles cheerfully.

'Lunch is off.'

'No matter. A few sandwiches will do me. I live here, so I'm entitled to something. The place looks as if it could do with a few customers. You should be full at this time of the year. Or perhaps you don't care whether you have any customers or not.'

'What do you mean by that?' demanded Brunner.

'Why bother with customers when there are easier ways of making money.'

'Such as?'

'Well, shark-fishing for instance.'

'I don't go in for it.'

'Your brother does.'

After a pause Brunner went on. 'Your name's Bigglesworth, I believe.'

'That's right.'

'I understand you're something to do with Scotland Yard!'

'Your information is correct.'

'Are you here on business or pleasure?'

'At the moment, strictly business. Does that worry

you?'

'No. Why should it? How much longer are you likely to be here?'

'Not much longer, I hope, I've nearly finished what I came to do, so by tomorrow I should be away. You might ask your brother to have my bill ready. I've merely looked in for a few sandwiches to take with me.'

'We don't do sandwiches.'

'I see you're having cold chicken. A little of that would suit me fine. Sorry to interrupt your lunch, but if you'll get someone to put a few slices between some bread and butter I'll be on my way. I'll take two packets, one for a friend.'

Brunner scowled, but he rang the bell on his table. When the waitress appeared he ordered the sandwiches. Looking at Biggles he said: 'You'll have to wait for my brother to make out your bill. He does the books. At present he's out fishing.'

'Not a good day for it, I'm told. Still, no doubt he'll bring a fish to show that his time wasn't wasted.'

With his eyes on Biggles' face Brunner said: 'What do you mean by that?'

Biggles answered. 'I think you know what I mean. I know all about your fishing activities, Mr Brunner. They're about to end.'

At this juncture the waitress came in with two packets of sandwiches. She put them on the table near which Biggles was standing and went out. Biggles picked up the packets.

'Thank you,' he said. 'Now I'll be going.'

'You're not going anywhere,' Brunner said coldly. 'You're staying here. Sit down.'

Biggles found himself looking into the muzzle of a small automatic pistol. He shook his head sadly. 'Oh really, Mr Brunner, what sort of nonsense is this? You've been looking at too much television. The things they do don't always work in real life. I have some friends outside, and if I don't soon join them they'll be in to see what I'm doing. You're in enough trouble as it is without making matters worse. You'd better start thinking about your position.'

'Can't we settle this between ourselves?' Brunner said with a hint of desperation in his voice. 'I'm a rich man.'

'So I believe; and I know why. I don't like that sort of money, so if you're offering me a bribe there's nothing doing. You've had your fun and before long you'll have to take your medicine. Good day to you.' Biggles turned and walked out of the room, wondering why he had given Brunner such a broad hint of what was afoot.

In a few minutes he had rejoined the others in the car.

'Some grub for you,' he said, handing Bertie his packet of sandwiches.'

'Any trouble in getting them?' asked Bertie.

'Not really,' answered Biggles evenly.

'The Auster has just gone over.'

'Good,' said Biggles.

They waited, eating their sandwiches in silence.

Chapter 14

THE SEA TAKES CONTROL

The plan began to develop. The Auster could be seen returning. Algy came through on the radio to say he had spotted the alleged fishing launch well out to sea on a course either for France or the island he had previously marked. As it still had a long way to go, he was returning to base rather than burn petrol for no reason and perhaps make it obvious to the enemy what he was doing. He would resume watching later, after he had refuelled.

Shortly after this the coastguard cutter appeared round the headland and turned into the harbour.

By this time it had been arranged that Biggles and Bertie should go with it, the two senior officers having decided to remain in the car to wait events and at the same time be in a position to keep in touch with their headquarters, by telephone, should it become necessary. Biggles and Bertie went down to the quay, and having introduced themselves were taken on board the patrol boat, a powerful, robust craft of about twenty tons, named the *Sea Scout*, with a crew of four including the engineer. There was no delay and in a matter of minutes the cutter, with a dinghy lashed on deck, was heading out to sea in a stiffening breeze.

Biggles joined the officer in charge, who was at the wheel, and turned out to be a retired Chief Petty Officer of the Royal Navy. He was a bearded man of late middle age. He said his name was Cole – Frank Cole.

'You must be wondering what all this is about,' began Biggles.

'I am,' was the reply. 'What's the trouble? I didn't get much of a briefing. I was simply told you were police officers from Scotland Yard and I was to put myself at your disposal to make a fairly long trip. You would give me the details.'

Biggles explained the situation. 'My assistants will be along in a plane, when the time comes, to mark the island for us,' he concluded.

'This cabin cruiser we're after must be the *Shearwater*,' said the sailor thoughtfully.

'Do you know it?'

'Sure I know it. I know all the small craft along our stretch of coast. I've often thought its behaviour was a bit off the normal. In fact, I've had a check on it once or twice. But it usually came back with a shark on board, so it seemed to be doing an honest job. Anyway, I couldn't find anything wrong. I must admit I didn't think of smuggling in human freight.'

'I don't think they wasted much time fishing, although for the look of it they sometimes brought a shark home with them. I believe they sometimes made the same fish serve for two or three trips.'

'Well I'll be damned!' exclaimed Cole wrathfully. 'So that's how they took me in.'

'Well, now you can get your own back,' replied Biggles cheerfully. 'We want to question the two men on the island, if they're still there, and everyone on board the *Shearwater*. That may include two bank robbers who are aiming to get abroad with a load of stolen money. As I see it they'd be put ashore on the island to be picked up in due course by a boat from the other side of the Channel. I think there must be two boats engaged in this racket, one from each side, but I'm only interested in the one that's been operating from Cornwall. When I'm more sure of my ground, I'll give our French friends the tip as to what's been going on and leave their side to them.'

'I only hope that when we get to the island we shall be able to get ashore,' Cole said.

'Do you know this particular island, then?'

'Not necessarily. But I shall know the area. I doubt if anyone knows every one of the Channel Islands.'

'Is there any reason why we shouldn't go ashore?'

'I'm looking at the weather. The report isn't too good. They say there's wind on the way. Getting ashore on these smaller islands with a sea running is always tricky, even for a dinghy,' Cole grinned. 'I hope you're a good sailor. We may have a rough passage. By the time we get to mid-Channel we shall know.'

For the next two hours nothing happened; that is, nothing to affect the operation except that the sea became steadily more turbulent, although this did not affect the performance of the revenue boat which had been designed for such conditions. Surprisingly, Biggles thought, they saw few ships, in what is reckoned to be one of the busiest shipping lanes in the world. Then, through flying spray, he made out a smaller craft ahead of them.

'That's the *Shearwater*,' observed Cole. 'I'd know her anywhere. She has no business, no legitimate business, anyhow, as far over as this.'

'She isn't on legitimate business,' reminded Biggles.

'I can overhaul her any time you like.'

'Better not get too close, yet, or they make take fright

and run for one of the larger islands,' advised Biggles.

Time went on, with the weather still deteriorating. The *Shearwater*, still a long way ahead, being smaller, was being tossed about, but showed no signs of turning back.

'I hope they're enjoying themselves,' muttered Biggles. 'How much further have we to go?'

'If I'm right about the island we're supposed to be making for, I'd say half an hour, give or take a few minutes. What happens if when they get to the island they find it's too rough to make a landing?'

'Do you think it will be too rough?'

'I'd say yes.'

'In that case the only thing we could do would be to follow the boat back to Cornwall and pick 'em up when they step ashore,' replied Biggles. The sound of an aero engine made him look up and he saw the Auster going over. 'There go my lads,' he told Cole. 'They'll mark the island for us when they see for certain which one it is. That's as much as they'll be able to do.'

'I wonder you didn't use a helicopter for this job,' remarked Cole. 'There are plenty in Cornwall, doing one job or another.'

'Yes. I know. But there were objections. A chopper may be all right if you know exactly what you're going to ask it to do. I was told that the island was mostly a lot of jagged rocks. Then there was the possibility of bringing back prisoners. Taking it by and large, a boat seemed a more reliable proposition.'

'What are your boys doing?' asked Cole, his eyes on the aircraft. 'They appear to be turning back.'

'Maybe they think that now we've got the enemy under observation we've no further use for them,' surmised Biggles. 'It might be a good idea, now, if we got a bit closer in case they tried to give us the slip in one of these squalls.'

'I'll see they don't do that,' Cole answered.

The cutter increased its speed until its bows were cleaving the angry water like a knife; and it was not long before a dark shadow, low in the water, came into view. 'That must be the island they're making for,' Biggles said. Actually, little could be seen of it yet for breakers that were flinging clouds of white spray high into the air. But as they drew nearer some details appeared.

The island, or perhaps more correctly islet, did not make an attractive picture by any standards. It might have been the back of a sea monster rising from the water had it not consisted almost entirely of chaotic water-worn rock. There was practically no vegetation, merely a few patches of coarse grass. Trees there were none. They were represented by a single hawthorn shrub, gnarled, its branches distorted and forced by the wind to crouch at an angle of thirty degrees to the ground.

'Not my idea of a desert island, old boy,' remarked Bertie. 'We shan't find any bananas here – if you see what I mean.'

'Nor anything else, by the look of it,' murmured Biggles, peering ahead through the flying spray.

'I'll tell you this,' said Cole soberly. 'Anyone trying to get ashore here today would be asking for trouble.'

'It looks as if the people ahead are going to have a shot at it,' returned Biggles. 'That's understandable. They must have seen us and realised we're after them. They'll do anything rather than be caught red-handed with a load of stolen money on board.'

'If they've been here before they may know of a sheltered spot under the wind,' Cole said. 'I hope you're not going to ask me to risk my ship by trying anything daft.'

'You may be sure I shan't ask you to do anything you don't consider reasonable,' answered Biggles with a bleak smile. 'And when I say that, I'm thinking as much of my own skin as your ship. I'm nothing for sea bathing in this sort of water.' He spoke with his eyes on the boat ahead, now in plain view. He went on. 'As I said just now, I imagine they'll take any chance to get away.'

'No doubt,' grunted Cole. He leaned forward, staring. 'Hello! What's this? Can you see what I see?'

Biggles looked. 'Another boat, by thunder!'

'Looks like a French fishing-boat. Coming up to the island from the far side. What do you make of it?'

Biggles thought for a few seconds. 'I'd say we're just in time to see a pick-up. I always realised this must be a two-way traffic, with the island a sort of half-way house. And there *is* a house of sorts, or a ruin,' Biggles went on, his voice rising. 'I can see it. Must be where men wait to be picked up. Yes, that's it. Two men have just come out. They're waving.'

There was a pause. Then Bertie, who was standing by and so far had said little, remarked: 'I'd bet they're not waving to us; and if it's the fishing-boat they're out of luck. It's turning away. It's just spotted us, and it doesn't like the look of us.'

'I guess you're right,' Cole said. 'Either they're not going to risk trouble with me, or they don't fancy getting any closer to the rocks in this sea; and I wouldn't blame 'em for that. We're too close ourselves for my liking.'

All three boats were now close to the island. Everything was in plain view, if sometimes half hidden by spray hurled high by crashing breakers. Overhead the Auster had circled back, apparently watching events to see how they would end. The French fishing-boat had turned back on its course. The *Shearwater* was still forging on; so was the *Sea Scout*, although at reduced speed.

Biggles said: 'It looks as if Brunner, or whoever is in charge of that boat, is going to try to get ashore. He must be desperate, seeing us on his tail. He won't want to jettison the loot he's got on board; or the crooks won't; they must know we shall be waiting for them if they go back to England. I'd bet there's a fine old argument going on aboard that craft.'

'It looks to me as if you're right,' answered Cole. 'They're going ashore at any cost. They're still going ahead, making, I think, for that gap between those two big rocks. They might find some shelter there out of the wind. All the same, they must be crazy. They must know that all the water round here bristles with rocks. I'm too close myself to feel comfortable.'

'If you feel like that I suggest we keep clear and leave these lunatics to do what they like,' Biggles said bluntly. 'It isn't worth taking a chance.'

Cole did not answer. Between anxious glances in the vicinity for tell-tale swirls over submerged rocks, he was trying to watch what the *Shearwater* was doing. Suddenly he burst out with: 'Great grief! I believe they've done it!'

No explanation was necessary. For a moment the boat in front had disappeared behind a curtain of spray; then it came into view beyond the two big rocks that acted as a natural breakwater.

'They were either smart or damned lucky,' stated Cole. 'I'm not going to try it. I need more water than they do. From the way they went in I reckon they must have done that before.'

Biggles did not speak. His eyes were on the *Shearwater*, which had run close to a great flat slab of rock that jutted at a downward slope into the sea like a ready-made slipway. Two suitcases were thrown ashore, to be followed instantly by the men who had thrown them. The two men already on the island ran forward to lend a hand. They snatched up the suitcases and reached forward to help the men, precariously poised to jump on the slippery, seaweed-festooned rock. They jumped, and fell. The boat began to turn away, turning as it did so, so that for a moment it lay, rocking, broadside on to the sea.

It was at this critical moment that disaster struck. It came in the form of a freak wave, one of those towering walls of water that can occur in a turbulent sea, that did the mischief. Rearing up, foam crested, it poured through the gap between the two protecting rocks like an avalanche, to crash in a smother of surf that blotted everything from view. When it subsided there was no one in sight: but the *Shearwater* was still there, lying half in and half out of the water across the end of the slipway.

'Now what?' asked Biggles in a tense voice. 'It looks as if she's had it.'

'Another big wave might wash her off, although whether she'd float or sink would depend on how badly she's been damaged. She may have been holed.' Cole went on. 'There's one thing certain. There's nothing we can do about it. Nothing would induce me to try to get in there. It'd be stark raving madness to attempt it. I'm not throwing my ship away for a bunch of crooks.'

'Those men may be drowning,' Biggles said

dubiously.

'That's no reason why we should drown with 'em,' returned Cole harshly. 'They knew what they were doing. We couldn't hope to get the boat off that slab of rock if we went in. She'll be high and dry at low tide, although she might come off in high tide. I'm not a life-boat or a salvage vessel. I'll report what has happened and leave it ot someone else to say what's to be done.'

Biggles didn't know what to say. What Cole had said was plain common sense. For more reasons than one he didn't like the idea of abandoning the place, but it would be stupid to attempt the impossible. He looked at Bertie, his eyes asking a question. Bertie shrugged helplessly.

'Okay,' Biggles told Cole. 'It's up to you. You do what you like. The ship is your responsibility.'

'Then for a start we'll get to where there aren't too many teeth in the water,' returned Cole. 'This sort of position would give any sailor nightmares.'

Overhead the Auster was leading away, apparently making for home.

'I may fly over when the sea's gone down a bit to have a closer look at things,' Biggles said.

'The wind will probably drop with the tide,' answered Cole, spinning the wheel to turn. He ducked as something struck the superstructure with a stinging smack. 'What the devil was that?' he rapped out.

'I've heard that sort of noise before,' Bertie said. 'Sounded mighty like a bullet to me. Yes, there's the hole,' he added pointing. 'Keep your heads down, boys.'

'But who could be shooting at us?' questioned Cole, wide-eyed.

'Unless fish or seagulls have taken to carrying guns, which seems unlikely, there's only one answer to that,' replied Biggles dryly. 'Someone on the island is letting us know he doesn't like us. Either that or he thinks he can discourage us from coming closer.'

'I didn't hear a shot fired.'

'You wouldn't, what with our engine and the noise of the waves.'

'Have you got a gun?'

'Not on me. Have you?'

'No. We don't carry firearms.'

Biggles went on grimly. 'I'm obliged to the gunman for letting us know he carried that sort of ironmongery. If I come back here I hope I shall be in a position to return the compliment.'

Another bullet struck the boat, making a star on the windscreen.

'I can't see anyone,' said Cole, peering.

'I'm not going to try,' declared Biggles. 'I've learned that when lead is flying it's a good plan to show as little of myself as possible.'

'He's got a nerve, shooting at us,' growled Cole.

'As we can't serve any useful purpose in hanging about here, giving him the opportunity, I suggest we move out of range,' Biggles said. 'That last shot came pretty close to your head.'

'You're dead right,' muttered Cole, putting on speed. Presently he went on: 'Do you want me to bring you back here when the sea quietens down?'

Biggles hesitated. 'That will need thinking about. I may decide to ask my Chief for orders. Meantime let's get home.'

There were no more shots: or if there were nothing was heard of them. They were soon out of range.

'That's better,' Biggles said. He looked up, but the Auster had faded into the murk that lay to the north.

Chapter 15

COLE MAKES A SUGGESTION

For a little while nothing more was said. Then Cole, who had appeared to be thinking, came out with: 'Is there anywhere in particular you'd like me to take you?'

Biggles answered: 'If it's all the same to you, I'd like to be put ashore at Polcarron. I shall have to go there to let my Chief know what has happened. Had you anywhere else in mind?'

'That depends on whether you want me to bring you back here later on.'

'What's the point of coming back here if this weather persists?'

'It won't. The wind's dropping, so the sea will soon go down. The barometer is rising, which should mean fair weather on the way. I imagine you don't want these crooks to get away with it.'

'I certainly do not.'

'Neither do I, after the way they've been pulling wool over my eyes.'

'Have you an alternative suggestion?'

'It struck me that if you intended coming back to this confounded island, there would be no point in going all the way to Cornwall. It'd be a waste of time.'

'Where else could we go?'

'We might run only as far as Jersey and wait there. We could be there in half an hour. It'd still be daylight.'

'That's an idea,' Biggles said approvingly. 'Could you do that?'

'I don't see why not. I could ring my headquarters to let them know what I was doing. St Helier would be handy for running back here if the weather was right. I see only one snag about that – at least, as far as you're concerned.'

'What is it?'

'There's at least one man on the island with a gun, and he's shown us he's prepared to use it. You say you're unarmed.'

'He's not to know that.'

'Does that mean you're prepared to take him on?'

'I've handled more difficult propositions. Bluff can work wonders.'

'Okay, if you feel like that. It's up to you.'

Bertie put in a word. 'Hold hard, chaps,' he said brightly. 'There's an airport on Jersey.'

Biggles answered. 'What's the use of an airport without an aircraft?'

'We could soon have one. What's wrong with ringing Morven from Jersey to tell the boys to bring the Auster over? There's a brace of pistols in the locker.'

Biggles smiled. 'Good for you. There are moments when you get an inspiration, and this is one of them. With the Auster I could slip over and have a look at the island before we tackled it. The trouble may be getting Algy or Ginger on the phone.'

'Why? They should be home by now, or they will be by the time we get to Jersey. Anyhow, there's bound to be someone at the clubhouse able to pass on a message.'

'We ought to let the Air Commodore know we're not coming back tonight,' Biggles said.

'If we can contact Algy he can let him know. You can tell Algy what has happened and he can pass it on.'

Biggles smiled again. 'True enough. The sea air must

be good for you.' He returned to Cole, now on a course for Jersey. 'How do you feel about all this? I mean, about putting us ashore on the island in the morning if the weather turns fair. The rocks will still be there.'

'They wouldn't worry me in a calm sea, because with the tide out I'd be able to see 'em. I needn't go right in. At a pinch you could go ashore in the dinghy, although with someone shooting at you that could be a bit tricky.'

'We'll jump that fence when we come to it,' replied Biggles. 'Okay, then. Let's see how it works out. It goes against the grain to return home empty-handed.'

'Right you are,' Cole said. 'If that's settled, let's get to Jersey for a start.'

There the conversation ended. The run to Jersey was uneventful and it was still broad daylight when the *Sea Scout* cruised into the harbour at St Helier, to take up a berth under the direction of the Harbour-Master. Saying he would see them later, Cole went ashore to telephone his head office in Falmouth. 'Where are you fellows going to spend the night?' he asked, as Biggles and Bertie followed him ashore. 'I shall probably stay on board,' he added.

'Don't worry about us,' Biggles answered. 'We shall manage.'

'I shall be on board if you want me.'

'Fair enough.'

Biggles and Bertie took a taxi to the airport, no great distance, to make arrangements for the Auster to land. This of course was facilitated by the presentation of his credentials. It took a little while to get a reply from Morven on the public telephone and then it was the assistant club secretary who answered. He said Ginger was there, having a drink and something to eat; he would fetch him; which he did. Then followed a long conversation with Ginger, although Biggles did most of the listening. Bertie, with increasing concern, was able to judge from Biggles' expression that he was receiving news that surprised him.

When, finally, Biggles hung up, Bertie asked impatiently: 'What was all that about?'

'Just a minute while I get it sorted out,' protested Biggles. 'Algy isn't there.'

'Not there! Where is he?'

'Gone to London.'

'What on earth for?'

'To take the Air Commodore back to town. Apparently while he was waiting the Chief put a call through to the Yard and was given news that decided him to go back. He took my car to the aerodrome, dropping the Chief Constable on the way, and was there, waiting, when the boys got back from their trip to the island. Algy took him straight on to London, leaving Ginger to hold the fort in case we came through. You see how things can come unstuck when people don't do what they say they're going to do,' concluded Biggles bitterly.

'Does that mean our scheme is off?'

'No. Ginger knows where we are and that we want the machine. As soon as Algy comes in he'll tell him and they'll come straight on here. The trip shouldn't take them more than half an hour. The regular services do it in forty minutes from Heathrow. Provided Algy isn't delayed anywhere, they should still get here before dark.'

'Does this mean your car is still at the airfield?'

'I suppose so, unless it can be arranged for someone to take it back to Polcarron. Not that it matters. As we shall probably fly back in the Auster when we're finished here, the car may as well be at the aerodrome as anywhere.'

'And what do we do now?'

'Wait for the Auster to arrive. There's nothing else we can do. I told Ginger we'd be here to meet them. We'll get some sandwiches to eat while we're waiting.'

They were able to make themselves comfortable on one of the seats in the big hall, which was just as well, for the wait turned out to be a long one. In fact, it was nearly dark when they heard the familiar purr of the Auster's engine, and the plane, having received permission to land from the control tower, came in, to be guided to its parking place by one of the staff, near other privately owned light planes that were kept at the airport.

'You've been a long time getting here,' accused Biggles, when they were together in the waiting hall.

'Have a heart,' protested Algy. 'I've been in the air nearly all day.'

'Tell me what happened,' requested Biggles, as they sat down.

'That won't take long,' stated Algy. 'We saw what happened this morning at the island and then went home. No trouble about that. When we got back we found the Air Commodore on the airfield waiting for us, having used your car to get there. He said he had to get to his office as quickly as possible – he didn't say why – so I flew him to Gatwick. That's all. When I got back to Morven Ginger told me you wanted the machine here, so here we are.'

'You told the Air Commodore what happened at the island?'

'As much as I could see from the air. He didn't seem too pleased at the way things had turned out; said he'd have to leave it to you to finish the job as best you could. He also said something about sending Inspector Gaskin down with a search warrant to go through Brunner's house at Penlock. Of course, he didn't know anything about you coming here. Neither did I at the time. What's the next move in this crazy business?'

'We couldn't land on the island this morning, the sea was too rough. So we're going back first thing tomorrow. The boat is in the harbour at St Helier. Before that I may make a quick reconnaissance in the Auster to see if there's any sign of life or activity. That shouldn't take long. Which reminds me. There are a couple of pistols in the locker. Don't let me go without them. In fact, Ginger, you might slip across now and fetch them, with two or three clips of ammunition, to make sure they aren't forgotten when we go to the boat.'

Ginger went off.

Algy said: 'So the idea is, you'll have a look at the island first thing in the morning, and if the sea is okay we'll all go along in the coastguard boat?'

'That's it; but I don't know about us all going on the boat. Cole, the skipper, may have something to say about that. He's a nice chap. But we can talk about this when the time comes.'

Ginger returned with the two small automatics always carried in the locker of the Auster for emergencies. Biggles put one in his pocket and handed the other one to Bertie.

'Are we going to stay here all night?' Ginger wanted to know.

'You can please yourselves, but I shall,' informed Biggles. 'I want to be in the air by dawn, so it's hardly worth while looking for quarters. I shall be all right here. I've slept on harder beds. The rest of you can take a taxi into the town. There are always some standing outside. I'll meet you on the quay at St Helier at, say, five o'clock. It'll be broad daylight by then. Let's hope the weather stays fair. That's the important thing.'

'If you're staying here, old boy. I'll stay with you,' volunteered Bertie. 'You'll do better in the morning with a second pair of eyes.'

'Okay, thanks, if that's how you feel,' returned Biggles. 'You may be right.'

Algy got up. 'Right. If that's settled I'll go with Ginger to St Helier and find some place where I can get a meal and put my feet up for an hour or two. Come on, Ginger.' And with that they departed.

Biggles settled himself on the seat. 'What a life,' he yawned. 'Why did I get myself bogged down in this business? It's time I had my head examined. That's the trouble with having a memory. If I hadn't recognised Limpy Logan on the quay at Polcarron, I might at this moment have been snug in my own little bed.'

Bertie smiled but said nothing. He, too, settled down to snatch some rest.

Chapter 16

GRUESOME DISCOVERIES

It was a few minutes before five the following morning when Biggles and Bertie, back from their dawn re-connaissance, stepped out of a taxi at St Helier and made their way to the quay where the *Sea Scout* was moored. They found Algy and Ginger already there, waiting, talking to Cole, who had been right in his forecast of the weather. It was near perfect; the sea dead calm with hardly a breath of wind.

'Well, what did you see?' asked Cole, who had been told what Biggles and Bertie were doing.

'Nothing worth talking about,' answered Biggles. 'Nobody moving on the island. The tide's left the *Shearwater* practically high and dry on that slab of rock. No one appears to have done anything about it.'

'Which probably means she's knocked a hole in her bottom,' conjectured Cole.

'The only craft in sight was a boat, not much larger than a rowing-boat, with one man in it. As far as I could make out he was hauling up lobster pots; nothing to do with us, anyway.'

'No sign of that French fishing-boat that made off yesterday when it saw us coming?'

'Not when we were there a few minutes ago.'

'Good. We don't want any trouble with France. They're a bit touchy about who owns some of these islands. Got a gun?'

'Yes. But I hope it won't be necessary to use it.'

'Very well. If everyone's ready we might as well be on our way,' Cole said.

'Just a minute,' requested Biggles, looking at Algy and Ginger in turn. 'I've been thinking about the plane, and decided someone ought to stay with it. Moreover, I haven't had time to do it myself, but someone ought to ring the Air Commodore to let him know what we're doing – in case of accidents. Which of you will stay? Perhaps you'd like to toss a coin for it?'

'There's no need for that,' replied Algy. 'Ginger can go if he wants to. I'll stay here. I'd as soon take a day off to rest my weary bones as go wild-goose hunting on the briny ocean.'

'Fair enough,' agreed Biggles. 'You may be right about hunting wild geese. We shall see. You can amuse yourself getting the Auster's tanks topped up ready for going home.' Turning to Cole he said, 'Okay, skipper. We're ready if you are.'

'Then let's get away. There may be a fuss if I'm absent for too long. We don't want the R.A.F. to turn out to search for us.'

The *Sea Scout* cast off and having cruised quietly to the open sea set a course for the island without a name.

The trip was uneventful up to the time the low-lying mass of rock crept up over the horizon. Not that there was any reason to expect trouble on the way. Any fishing-boats that had been out overnight had presumably gone home with their catch. Nor, as they drew closer, could the little boat, which Biggles had thought was lobstering, be seen. Once, for a few minutes, one of the regular service planes announced its presence as it headed south for one of the French coastal landing grounds, with a load of people going on holiday.

As the island rose higher from the now dead calm sea,

Cole handed Biggles his binoculars. 'I can't see anything. Perhaps you can.'

Biggles spent a minute surveying the islet. 'No,' he said. 'Nobody moving. Maybe they can see us coming and have gone into hiding. I can see the *Shearwater*. She still appears to be fast on the rock where she went ashore.'

'Maybe waiting for dead low tide to check for damage,' guessed Cole. 'Otherwise, if she was holed it'd be no use hauling her off. She'd only go to the bottom. If she's all right they may be able to rock her off at high tide. If they can't, unless they have some food available they'll be only too glad to be taken off. Some of these smaller islands aren't visited for weeks, or even months on end.'

Ginger spoke. 'Be a bit of an anti-climax if we found nobody here at all.'

'There's bound to be someone, unless that French fishing-boat we saw came over during the night and took everyone off. I reckon there should be at least six men here. Stephen Brunner and his chauffeur Bates, with the two men they had with them; and the two were already here waiting to be picked up, to be put ashore in Cornwall.'

'We're only assuming that the French fishing-boat we saw had anything to do with the racket,' Cole pointed out. 'It may have come over to look at some lobster pots.'

'Then why should it make off when it saw us?' asked Biggles.

'It wouldn't want to be caught lobstering round British islands. There's been a spot of bother more than once about that sort of thing. You're not allowed to poach round somebody else's property,' stated Cole.

'Why worry,' put in Bertie. 'We shall soon know all about it.'

This was a logical remark, because the *Sea Scout* was now coming up, at half speed, to its objective. Cole did not have to explain the reason for the reduced speed. It was all too obvious. With the tide well out, seaweed-covered rocks were showing above water in several places. Still there was no sign of anyone on the isand; but Cole, his eyes on the rocks, advanced with increasing caution.

At last he said. 'This is as close as I feel inclined to go. Perhaps you wouldn't mind going ashore in the dinghy.'

'Suits me,' agreed Biggles. 'A few yards at the oars shouldn't do us any harm.'

'I'll stand by in case you have to come back in a hurry,' promised Cole. 'This is your show, so I'll leave you to handle it as you think best.'

Without any more ado the dinghy was put on the water. Biggles, Bertie and Ginger got into it. Bertie and Ginger picked up the oars. Biggles, taking the rudder, steered for the gap between the two big rocks where the *Shearwater* had gone in. Knowing there was, or had been, a gunman on the island, his eyes roved the shore; but the only sign of life were the gulls that greeted the approach of the intruders with loud cries of disapproval.

The dinghy's keel scraped on a little beach of shingle and broken rock not far from where the *Shearwater* lay on her side. Shipping their oars, Bertie and Ginger jumped out and hauled the dinghy to where it was not likely to move. Biggles joined them, still regarding with suspicion the rocks above them. When nothing happened he turned his eyes to the high water mark, the usual line of rubbish; seaweed, orange peel old ice-cream cartons and the like, left by the receding tide. Conspicuous were a number of small pieces of paper.

'Looks as if some silly asses have been having a paperchase,' remarked Bertie casually.

'For a start we'll have a look at the wreck,' Biggles said.

As they walked slowly towards it he went on: 'What is all this stuff?' and so saying picked up one of the pieces of loose paper. He looked at it. Stopped. Started at it. 'Well, what do you know?' he breathed. 'Take a look at this.' He held the paper for the others to see. It was an English five pound note.

Ginger whistled. 'So we've struck treasure island at last?' he cried, grinning, looking along the line of scraps of paper.

'Lovely money,' declared Bertie. 'Let's collect it. Every man for himself – what?'

'Just a minute,' ordered Biggles curtly. 'Don't get excited. I can see what's happened here.'

'Sticks out a mile, old boy,' Bertie said. 'One of the suitcases was bust open when that big wave bashed it on the rocks.'

'That's the answer,' agreed Biggles. He looked up and down the high water mark. 'But where's the suitcase? It should be here. In fact, there were two suitcases.'

'Somebody must have been here before us,' offered Ginger.

'That's what it looks like,' confirmed Biggles. 'Whoever it was he may still be here, so watch out. Never mind the money. That can wait. Let's have a look at the wreck. I have a feeling we're not alone here, so keep your eyes skinned and be ready to move fast

Somebody may be waiting for us to come into range to have a crack at us.'

Cautiously they advanced towards where the cabin cruiser lay on its beam ends with the stern just in the water. Suddenly Biggles pulled up dead, holding out a warning hand. 'Hello! What's all this?' he exclaimed, pointing at the ground, in particular at an ugly stain.

'Looks like blood to me,' Ginger said.

'And me. There's been dirty work here.' Biggles' eyes were following a faint trail of bloodstains. They led in the direction of the wreck. Slowly, alert, he began to follow it. He had only taken a few paces when he stooped to pick up a small pocket automatic. He handed it to Ginger. 'You may need that,' he said, meaningfully, and walked on to the boat, to sidestep smartly as an object lying behind it came into view. It was a body.

'That's Bates, the chauffeur,' Bertie said, coming up. 'He won't hurt us. He won't hurt anyone any more. He's dead. I'd say he was drowned when that big wave caught them. The backwash would drag him back into the water. Maybe the poor blighter couldn't swim.'

'He never had a chance. Look at his head. He was either knocked out or killed on the spot when that wave threw him against the rock. He was washed up afterwards. Well, that's one accounted for.' Biggles climbed up the sloping side of the boat and looked down into the cabin. 'Good grief!' he cried. 'Here's another one.'

'Who is it?'

'Brunner.'

'Dead?'

'Looks like it. Wait.' Biggles scrambled down into the cabin. He was soon back. 'He's dead all right,' he reported. 'But he wasn't drowned. He was shot. Bearing in mind the blood on the beach, this begins to make sense. There's been murder done here. That's something I didn't expect. We shall have to watch our step.'

'Where are the others?' Ginger said.

'That's something we shall have to find out,' returned Biggles. 'I think Brunner must have been shot on the beach, but managed to get to the boat, where he died. It may have been his pistol we picked up, he having dropped it when he was hit.'

'What's that lying along there, tangled up with that mass of seaweed?' Bertie was pointing. 'Is it a man or a log?'

They walked along to the object. It was a man, unknown to any of them. No wound could be found, so he appeared to have been drowned. 'That's three,' Biggles said. 'We're doing fine,' he added with grim honour. 'There must have been a battle here, probably over the money.'

'There are still three more,' reminded Ginger.

Biggles raised a hand, his head in a listening attitude. 'Listen! Did you hear something?'

'Seagull,' said Bertie.

'Sounded to me more like someone calling for help,' opined Ginger.

'Where did it come from?'

'Over here, I think, among those rocks.' Bertie started walking inland.

'Watch how you go,' warned Biggles, his eyes busy on the skyline. 'There's a murderer not far away. He can't get away. The *Shearwater* has got a fair-sized hole below the water line.'

A groan from the rocks brought them all to a halt.

Then Biggles, pistol in hand, walked on again. 'Watch it,' he said tersely. 'This may be a trap. Here we are,' he went on quickly, hurrying forward.

Between the rocks a man was lying as if he had fallen. He was about fifty years of age, dressed in stained blue overalls. His face was chalk white, making a heavy black moustache the more conspicuous. Biggles went up to him. 'Who are you?' he asked curtly. Then, in a quick aside: 'This place is looking more like a battlefield every minute.'

The man looked at him uncomprehending. '*Parlez-vous française, m'sieur?*'

'*Oui.* Who are you and where are you from?' asked Biggles, in French.

The man said he was a French fisherman from St Malo.

'What are you doing here.'

The man admitted he had come hoping to catch some lobsters.

'You came here alone?'

'*Oui, monsieur.*'

'What's the matter with you?'

The man said he had been shot.

'Where?'

The man pointed to his groin.

'Who shot you, and why?'

The man said he didn't know. He looked as if he was speaking the truth. 'Men were here. There was a battle,' he explained, wincing with pain.

To the others Biggles said: 'We'd better see how badly he's hurt. He's lost a lot of blood by the look of him.' He examined the wound. A glance showed the man had not lied. It was serious but not likely to be fatal if he could be got to a hospital. With their combined handkerchiefs Biggles did as much as was possible in the circumstances. With a wad and a tight bandage he stopped the bleeding after which the man seemed more comfortable.

'This is a complication,' Biggles told the others, looking worried. 'We can't just leave him lying here. Somehow we shall have to get him to our boat. For that we shall need help.' To the wounded man he said: 'How did you get here?'

The man said he came in a small boat, his own.

'Where is it?'

'At the bottom of the sea.'

'How did that happen?'

The man told his story. He had landed on the island. Then he had heard shooting, so he had tried to see who was shooting and why. There were men fishing on the beach. There was a boat on the rocks. He was trying to run away when he had been shot. Then two of the men had tried to steal his boat; but they were bad sailors, and in trying to raise the sail the boat had capsized. He thought the men in it had been drowned. He didn't see them come ashore. He heard more shooting. Then he thought he must have fainted. That was all he knew.

'Who were these men you found here?' asked Biggles.

The man said he didn't know. He looked like fainting again from the effort of talking.

'We shall have to do something about this,' Biggles told the others. 'It means we shall have to get extra hands from the *Sea Scout*. We'll never manage to carry him alone.'

'What can Cole do about it?' questioned Ginger. 'He won't want to take the man to France. He'd be held there pending inquiries.

'We shall have to leave that to him,' Biggles said. 'He

might have a first-aid kit on board.'

'Hold hard, chaps!' exclaimed Bertie, who was looking at the *Sea Scout*, which had moved a little closer in. 'Somebody's waving a white towel; sending a signal, I think.'

'He's sending Morse,' observed Ginger.

Together they read the message. It was short and simple. 'French boat approaching from far side island.'

'That just about queers our pitch,' muttered Biggles angrily. 'It must be coming here by arrangement to pick up the two men Brunner brought here yesterday. As I understand it, the two men already here were waiting to be taken to England.'

'What can we do about it?' asked Bertie. 'If we try to stop 'em landing there's likely to be another shooting match.'

'Wait a minute,' Biggles rapped out. 'I've got an idea. This may suit us.'

'Tell me how, old boy, tell me how,' requested Bertie. 'I don't get it.'

Chapter 17

HOW IT ALL ENDED

Biggles explained what he had in mind. 'If the men on this French boat come ashore, as I imagine they will, we should be able to persuade them to take this poor fellow back to France. After all, he's one of them. He isn't a crook. His only sin was doing a little quiet poaching in British waters, and there's nothing outrageous about that. I suggest that Ginger stays here to look after him while Bertie comes with me to see if we can make contact with these other Frenchmen.'

This was thought to be a reasonable plan, one which, if it worked, would relieve them of their new responsibility. So Biggles and Bertie, knowing they couldn't have far to go, set off across the island. When they reached the highest part they could see what previously had been hidden from their view. The fishing-boat was close in, hauling down its single sail. They also saw something else. Two men were already on the scrap of sandy beach in a little cove for which the French boat was obviously making. One carried a suitcase. They were waving to those on the oncoming boat.

'Where's the third man?' said Bertie. 'There should be another. We've only seen two.'

'There shouldn't be any more if our wounded friend was right in assuming that the two who tried to pinch his boat were drowned,' Biggles pointed out. 'The fact that only one, the one we saw, was washed up on the beach is neither here nor there. The other may be on the bottom with the boat. We'll deal with those we can see.'

At this moment one of the men on the beach happened to look round, and, of course, saw Biggles and Bertie striding down the slope towards them. He said something to his companion, whereupon both men ran to the end of the little cove and disappeared behind some rocks.

'They must know we're from the coastguard cutter,' remarked Biggles. 'If they start shooting this won't be funny.' He continued to walk forward. This produced the report of a pistol shot. The bullet smacked against a rock some distance away, suggesting that the men who had fired was not very good with a pistol unless it was merely intended as a warning. Biggles fired an answering shot. 'We'll let him know that two can play at that game, if that's how they want it,' he growled.

There was no more shooting. Biggles and Bertie went on to the beach, and there, presently, the French boat arrived. Its name, and port of registration, St Malo, could be read. Biggles waved, remarking: 'As they come from the same place as our wounded friend, they may know him.'

Two men got out of the boat and waded ashore. There was no sign of hostility; but, of course, they could not have known the state of affairs on the island. Biggles walked forward to meet them and spoke to the first man to step on dry land. Speaking in French, he said he wanted to see the captain. They were British Government officers, he explained. On the island they had found a wounded Frenchman. He had been shot. Would they take him on board and put him ashore at St Malo, which was where he came from? It would be better, and quicker, than taking him to England. He had come to the island for lobsters, in his own boat, but it had been stolen.

As can be imagined, the men listened to this in wide-eyed astonishment. After staring at each other, one went back to the boat, now with its bows on the beach, and with much gesticulation held a conversation presumably with the captain, or the man in charge. He joined the others at the spot where Biggles and Bertie were standing waiting. Having announced himself to be the captain, he asked, naturally, what had happened on the island.

Biggles explained. He said he had nothing against the French boat, although the British police knew what had been going on. He himself was a police officer and the traffic would have to end, or there would be trouble. There had been murder done on the island. A man, a Frenchman who had taken no part in the trouble, had been wounded. He had dressed the wound, but could do nothing more. The man should be in hospital. He came from St Malo. Would the captain take him there?

The captain did not argue. *'Merci, m'sieur.'* He said he understood. 'Where is this wounded man?'

'Come, I will show you.'

The captain beckoned the two members of his crew, and the party, now five in number, with Biggles leading the way, trooped across the island.

When they arrived at the place where the wounded man lay, Ginger was sitting beside him. 'He's fainted,' he said. 'Loss of blood, I suppose.'

The captain recognised the sick man instantly, which was not surprising as they came from the same port. 'So it is Paul Voudray,' he said shortly. 'He lives near me. I warned him he would get into trouble one day if he came here alone.'

'Did he know what you were doing?'

'*Non, monsieur.*'

'Will you take him home?'

'*Mais certainement.*'

'And will you promise me never to come back?'

'On my honour, *m'sieur.*'

'There are two men here, waiting for you, I think. I will deal with them.'

The captain said he understood. That was all. The Frenchmen picked up their wounded compatriot and carried him to their boat. He was put on board. The captain said: '*Bonjour, monsieur, et merci.*' The boat pushed off. The sail was hoisted and it headed out to sea, towards France.

'That gets rid of one difficulty,' Biggles said thankfully. 'Ginger, dash back to Cole and let him know we're okay. We may be a few minutes.'

'Right,' said Ginger, and departed at a run.

'And now what?' enquired Bertie. 'What are you going to do about these two villains here?'

'I'll try to have a word with them,' replied Biggles. 'If they won't give themselves up, they can stay here till they starve to death or wait till someone else comes to fetch them. I'm not risking getting a bullet in my ribs in a place like this, not on your nellie.'

'I can see one of 'em squinting round a rock. Must be wondering what goes on.'

'I can see him.' Keeping well down, Biggles shouted: 'Hi, you. Can you hear me?'

'What do you want?' came back the answer.

'I want you. Are you coming quietly?'

'Go to hell. Come and get us.' This was followed by a pistol shot.

'Listen, you fools.' shouted Biggles. 'The game's up.

I'm giving you a chance. No more boats will come here. The Frenchmen have gone for good. Are you prepared to be stuck here for months, or will you pack it in?'

This was followed by a silence in which the men may have discussed their position. Presently one of them announced the decision. 'We're staying. Try getting us, copper.'

'Okay, if that's how you want it,' called Biggles. 'I hope you enjoy a diet of limpets and salt water.' He turned to Bertie. 'Come on, chaps. Let's get out of this. I'm in no mood for heroics.' So saying he started back across the island.

A shot followed them, but it did no damage.

They reached the cove to find Ginger waiting by the dinghy. 'Where are the crooks?' he asked.

'We're leaving them here to sweat it out,' Biggles told him. 'They can't get away, so it isn't worth taking chances. If by some stroke of luck they did get to France, they'd be arrested for attempted murder. The Frenchmen know all about them. Let's collect some of this money lying about. Cole can decide what to do with the bodies. He can put us off in Jersey and we'll press on home by air. When we've told the Air Commodore what's happened, he can do what he likes about it. Maybe get the Navy to take a hand. We've done as much as we could be expected to do.'

Having returned to the coastguard boat, he told Cole the story of events on the island. 'If you'll put us off at Jersey, I hope I shan't have to trouble you again,' he concluded.

Cole swore. 'I hate bodies on board, but I suppose I'd better take 'em, or the gulls may find 'em and spoil 'em for identification,' he grumbled.

'We'll give you a hand,' offered Biggles.

Which they did.

So it worked out. Within the hour the Air Police party stepped ashore at St Helier, leaving the coastguard to continue on their way to their home station. A taxi took them to the airport where they found Algy waiting. As soon as the usual formalities were completed Biggles took off, and two hours later he was in the Air Commodore's office reporting in detail the events of the day.

The Air Commodore heard him out without comment. Then he said: 'I think you did right in leaving those two men on the island. It wasn't worth risking your life for a couple of common crooks who, knowing they had nothing to lose, would not have hesitated to shoot you, given the chance. You can leave the rest to me. I'll have a word with the Admiralty about collecting them, and any money still lying about on the beach. It'll be an exercise for the boys in blue.'

'What about Brunner's brother – Julius? When I last saw him he was at The Fishermen's Arms,' Biggles said.

'You needn't worry about him. He won't give any more trouble.'

'Why not?'

'He's dead.'

'Dead! How did that happen?'

'He shot himself. I don't know what you told him, but apparently he realised the crooked business he and his brother had been running was all washed up and he couldn't face the consequences. Somehow he managed to get home to Penlock Grange. I had sent Inspector Gaskin down with a couple of men and a search warrant. Unable to get a reply, they had to break in. There was no one there except Julius Brunner and he lay dead on the library floor with a shotgun lying beside him. He had blown his brains out.'

'Silly fellow,' murmured Biggles sadly. 'He could have made plenty of money without turning to crime,' He shrugged. 'But some people are like that. They can never have enough. It seems a pity. I think his brother Stephen was the real culprit. He was a nasty piece of work.'

The Air Commodore got up. 'Well, there it is. You'd better go home and get some rest. You look tired. Anyhow, you have the satisfaction of knowing your hunch about what you saw at Polcarron was right on the beam.'

'The trouble with me is I see to much,' returned Biggles lugubriously, as he turned to the door. 'All I do is knock my pan out working overtime. I'll be more careful in future.'

He went on.

As the reader may feel somewhat 'left in the air' over one or two details, here is a note by way of a postscript.

It is unlikely that what exactly happened on the island when the bank robbers arrived with their haul will ever be known, although Biggles' interpretation of it was probably the true one. When the suitcase was burst open by the wave that wrecked the *Shearwater*, and its contents revealed, there was a fight between the newcomers, and those already on the island for possession of the bank-notes. This would be in accord with the characters of the men concerned. Stephen Brunner and his chauffeur had tried to intervene and had been shot for their pains. The same with the French lobster fisher, although it is quite possible that he was shot by accident.

Unfortunately, the two men who knew the truth, the two Biggles had left on the island, were not available for questioning, for when a party of marine commandoes arrived to collect them, they were no longer there; and it was some time before it was learned that they had been arrested by the French police for the attempted murder of the French fisherman from St Malo who had chosen an unlucky moment to visit his lobster pots.

The reason for the silence was no doubt due to the fact that the ownership of the barren mass of rock had long been in dispute. At all events, it came to the same thing in the end, in that the two men spent some years in a French prison instead of an English one. They were crooks who had been wanted for a long time.

Nor were any more bank-notes found on the beach. This was understandable, as they would be washed away at the next high tide. Certainly for some time afterwards there were whispers of English five-pound notes being picked up from the shores of holiday resorts on the larger islands.

With the deaths of the chief conspirators, at the inquest on Tom Draper, the barman at The Fishermen's Arms, a possible charge of murder had to be dropped. The verdict could only be 'accidental death'.

Taking the whole thing by and large, Biggles always regarded the case as having an unsatisfactory ending. But as Bertie on one occasion reminded him when the subject was raised: 'You can't always win, old boy, so you might as well forget it.'

If you have enjoyed this book you may like to read
some other exciting titles from Knight Books:

CAPTAIN W. E. JOHNS

BIGGLES LEARNS TO FLY
BIGGLES INVESTIGATES
BIGGLES BREAKS THE SILENCE
BIGGLES SEES TOO MUCH
BIGGLES AND THE PLOT THAT FAILED
BIGGLES AND THE DARK INTRUDER

Whether on holiday in Cornwall or on missions which take him as far away as the South Pole or the Sahara Desert, Biggles has an instinct for uncovering crime and rooting out villainy.

In these vivid and exciting stories, Biggles and his friends get involved in some of the most dangerous adventures of their careers. As always they face them with the courage and good sense which readers everywhere have come to associate with their favourite airborne heroes.

KNIGHT BOOKS

CHRIS POWLING

MOG AND THE RECTIFIER

Mog is the greatest leader a gang ever had; Mog's hero is the Rectifier. Mog's plans to follow in the footsteps of this mysterious Robin Hood figure are continually thwarted by spoilt rich-kid Howard Bygrave and his sinister chauffeur Mr Skin. By chance they all get involved with the Rectifier's plans and something that starts as a game suddenly becomes serious.

A tangle of crises develops and somehow the powerful, elusive figure of the Rectifier is behind it all . . .

KNIGHT BOOKS

ROBERT SWINDELLS

WORLD-EATER

One night after a violent storm a mysterious new planet appears in the sky. At first Orville Copperstone is too preoccupied with his pet pigeon to pay it much attention, but soon the whole world is buzzing with the news of this strange event.

Scientific probes begin to reveal incredible facts about this unique planet, but it is Orville who suddenly realises the dreadful truth about the planet's true nature. But will anyone believe *him*? And if they finally do, how can they prevent a seemingly inevitable disaster?

KNIGHT BOOKS

BARONESS ORCZY

THE SCARLET PIMPERNEL

Amidst the turbulence of the French Revolution, a mysterious and heroic Englishman – known as the Scarlet Pimpernel – snatches doomed aristocrats to safety from the very shadows of the guillotine.

Desperate to capture this daring stranger, the revolutionaries will go to any lengths – forcing even the woman he loves to betray '. . . that damned, elusive Pimpernel!'

KNIGHT BOOKS

MORE EXCITING KNIGHT BOOKS

Captain W. E. Johns
☐ 10249 5 BIGGLES INVESTIGATES £1.50

Captain W. E. Johns
☐ 10460 0 BIGGLES AND THE PLOT
THAT FAILED £1.50

Captain W. E. Johns
☐ 02464 X BIGGLES AND THE DARK
INTRUDER £1.75

Chris Powling
☐ 28046 8 MOG AND THE RECTIFIER 95p

Robert Swindells
☐ 32889 4 WORLD-EATER £1.25

Baroness Orczy
☐ 25621 4 THE SCARLET PIMPERNEL
£1.50

All these books are available at your local bookshop or newsagent, or can be ordered direct from the publisher. Just tick the titles you want and fill in the form below.

Prices and availability subject to change without notice.

Hodder & Stoughton Paperbacks, P.O. Box 11, Falmouth, Cornwall.

Please send cheque or postal order, and allow the following for postage and packing:

U.K. – 55p for one book, plus 22p for the second book, and 14p for each additional book ordered up to a £1.75 maximum.

B.F.P.O. and EIRE – 55p for the first book, plus 22p for the second book, and 14p per copy for the next 7 books, 8p per book thereafter.

OTHER OVERSEAS CUSTOMERS – £1.00 for the first book, plus 25p per copy for each additional book.

Name ....

Address ....

....